W9-BQZ-452

0 00 30 0205181 5

BRANCH

The Luckiest Girl in the World

Steven Levenkron

SCRIBNER

SCRIBNER
1230 Avenue of the Americas
New York, NY 10020

Copyright © 1997 by Lion's Crown, Ltd.
All rights reserved, including the right of reproduction in
whole or in part in any form.
SCRIBNER and design are trademarks of
Simon & Schuster Inc.

Designed by Brooke Zimmer
Set in Fairfield
Manufactured in the United States of America

1   3   5   7   9   10   8   6   4   2

Library of Congress Cataloging-in-Publication Data
Levenkron, Steven, date.
The luckiest girl in the world : a novel/Steven Levenkron.
p.   cm.
I. Title.
PS3562.E872L8   1997
813'.54—dc21   96-44353
                      CIP

ISBN 0-684-82604-6

For my wife, Abby,
and
my daughters Rachel and Gabrielle

ACKNOWLEDGMENTS

I gratefully acknowledge the assistance of Louise Shaffer in the preparation of this book.

I would also like to acknowledge the help that Greer Kessel has provided as my editor at Scribner. From her enthusiasm to her fastidiousness in reviewing the manuscript, her interest and support for this project were invaluable.

In addition, I would like to thank my agent, Olga Wieser at Wieser & Wieser, for bringing together author and publisher in both concept and detail.

The Luckiest Girl in the World

I

The music from her mom's old tape recorder filled the rink as Katie Roskova skated to the center of the ice. It was seven o'clock in the morning, and Katie had already been up for two hours. Every day her alarm clock went off promptly at five. By five-thirty she was in the kitchen swallowing a hasty breakfast while leaning over the sink so she wouldn't have to waste precious time cleaning up after herself. Ten minutes later she and her mother were on the road, driving from their home in New Rochelle to the skating rink in Hartford, Connecticut. Her mornings had been like this for as long as she could remember. Once in a while she'd hear other kids talk about sleeping until noon on a weekend or during a vacation. She couldn't imagine what that would feel like.

"When you wish upon a star, makes no difference who you are," sang Jiminy Cricket. "Anything your heart desires will come to you . . ."

But Jiminy had it all wrong. Only the winners got what their hearts desired, as Katie knew very well. "And that's why you're going to do it right," she told herself sternly. "You're not going to mess up—for once." "It" was her new long program for the junior championships, which she and her coach, Ron, were starting work on today. "Please, please let me be good," she prayed. "Let me be perfect."

"Stay nice and loose, Katie," Ron called out from the other side of the rink. "Don't try for any big drama moments." Katie nodded and struck her opening pose: back arched slightly, chin lifted, eyes gazing at something in the distance—just a sweet little ingenue. Big drama wasn't her thing—Mom and Ron had told her that over and over again. That was why the music for her program was a medley of Walt Disney songs. "It's simple and sweet," Mom had said when she picked it. "It's perfect for Katie's style." Katie wasn't convinced that simple and sweet was her style any more than big drama was, but there was no point in saying that to Mom. Besides, it was her job to be whatever was required.

"When your heart is in your dreams . . ." sang Jiminy.

"Remember, hands behind your back, Katie," Ron yelled.

Guiltily, Katie clasped her hands behind her back. "Way to go, stupid," jeered the voice inside her head. "You haven't even started, and already you've screwed up." But she pasted a smile on her face and took off with a long, curving stroke across the rink.

RON WATCHED Katie cover the ice with grace and skill. She was a pretty girl, petite and fragile-looking, with a heart-shaped face framed by a mane of wavy black hair. Her features were delicate, and her huge, dark eyes always seemed a little wistful to Ron. Until she smiled. The kid had a big smile that could carry to the back row of any arena. Ron stole a quick glance up to the bleachers where Katie's mother, Katherine, was sitting. From a distance mother and daughter looked remarkably alike. But when they stood side by side, there were some obvious differences. Katherine was taller and sturdier than her daughter; she had a vibrancy and power Katie lacked. No way you could ever say that Katherine Roskova was fragile. Ron turned his attention back to the ice and the girl who was skating to music from a movie about a little puppet who wanted a life without strings.

THE MUSIC SWOOPED and swelled. It was corny, Katie thought, but it was kind of sad too—funny Mom hadn't picked up on that, but then Mom never did pick up on the things she didn't want to know. Katie liked the sadness. She relaxed a little and let the bittersweet melody flow over her. Actually, she enjoyed skating the opening section of her program. Ron had choreographed it to take advantage of her strengths, so it was loaded with the spins and the graceful, balletic moves she did best. Later, she'd face the parts she didn't do well—the all-important, no-way-anyone-ever-wins-without-them jumps. The jumps she dreaded . . .

"Stop thinking like that, stupid," she commanded herself. "Focus on what you're doing, or you'll blow the easy part." She pushed the jumps out of her mind and concentrated on Jiminy singing. Soon her natural musicality took over and she skimmed over the ice gracefully—the picture of a sweet, simple girl skating to a song about dreams that came true.

IN THE BLEACHERS above the rink, Katherine Roskova was working hard to hold on to her temper. She hated the opening of this new program. It was boring, boring, boring. She knew the judges would hate it too—if they stayed awake long enough to watch it. The worst part was, there was nothing she could do about it. When she'd tried—very gently—to suggest to Ron that he should start with more pizzazz, he'd given her a lot of psychobabble about helping Katie build her confidence by letting her skate her best material first. The truth was, Ron coddled Katie. Katherine had called him on it once, but then she'd had to back down because he'd threatened to walk and she couldn't afford to start over with another coach. Now she was stuck with this dreary program. It was her hard-earned money that paid Mr. Sensitivity's coaching fees. She was the one who got up at the crack of dawn every day to schlep Katie to the rink for morning practice. She skipped her lunch hour so she could leave work early and get the girl back to the rink after school. She drove a car that was ten years old so she could afford custom-built skates; she went without new clothes so she could pay for extra rink time. So if she wanted pizzazz, then, damn it, she'd earned it. She shifted angrily in her seat. Down below her the slender figure on the ice executed a graceful spin. Katherine watched and the harsh lines in her face softened. Someday it would all be worth it, she thought. All the sacrifice and hard work would pay off someday.

In the medley, Jiminy Cricket had given way to Snow White, who was singing about the prince who would come someday. Katie stretched out her strokes to fill the phrases of the violins. In her mind she pictured a magical forest and a beautiful young girl waiting for her love.

IF ANYONE COULD play Snow White and get away with it, it was Katie, thought Ron. With her ethereal look, she was made for the role. Especially when she was skating freely and without pressure, the way she was right now. He skated around the perimeter of the rink so he could watch her without getting into her sight line and distracting her. At her best Katie reminded him of the great female skaters of the past—lyrical, elegant performers like Fleming and Hamill. Unfortunately, lyrical skating wasn't in anymore. Today it was all about jumping. Katie didn't have a big triple jump—there were times when she missed her doubles—and he wasn't sure she'd ever have the kind of athletic strength necessary to develop one. Still, you never knew. For all her fragile prettiness, Katie was a tough little jock. He'd seen her skate through falls, injuries, and fatigue without a whimper. She might just push herself hard enough to get those jumps. The pity was, she'd never be as lovely to watch as she was right now.

KATIE FELT AS IF she were flying. The cold air filled her lungs, and her skating skirt fluttered in the breeze around her body. Only her skate blades were working as they cut long arcs in the ice. For a moment the harsh voice in her head was quiet and her mind seemed to take off—almost the way it did when she spaced out, she thought dreamily. It was strange, because she hadn't had any of the warning signs, but she was feeling exactly the same . . . Suddenly, she realized with horror what she was thinking, and stopped herself so violently she almost fell. Because spacing out—and everything that went along with it—was her guilty secret. It was something she must never let happen—never even let herself think about—when she was skating.

Shaken, she tried to regain the momentum she'd lost when she'd almost stumbled.

"Stupid," railed the voice inside her head. "Stupid, stupid, stupid."

And now, as if she didn't have enough problems, the jumps were coming up.

RON CAUGHT THE glitch in Katie's stroke and attributed it to nerves. Her first jump—a double toe loop—was next. This wasn't a good sign, he thought. If the mere thought of the toe loop was spooking her, they were in big trouble. He skated closer to her.

UP IN THE BLEACHERS, Katherine felt her own legs and feet pushing against the floor as if she were Katie digging her skates into the ice. Katherine had loved working on jumps when she skated. Not that she'd ever gotten to anything like Katie's level of skill—there was no way she could have when she was young. Her parents had been too poor and ignorant to even consider skating lessons for her. She leaned forward intently. The jump that was coming up wasn't easy, but Katie could pull it off. She had to.

KATIE TURNED ONTO her back edge and started to build her speed for the toe loop. Her blades cut the ice fast and deep. "Please let me do it, please let me do it right," she repeated in her head like a mantra. Ron was skating behind her. Her mom was watching from the bleachers. As Katie reached back with the toe of her left skate for the launch, she could feel them both holding their breaths. "Please," she prayed, "please." She pulled herself up off the ice. Her height was good. She could almost hear Mom sigh with relief. But in the air she felt the jump go sour. She knew she didn't have the rotation for a double.

"Single it, Katie," Ron called out.

"Loser!" the voice inside her head screamed. "Loser, loser, loser!"

"Single it," Ron called again. But she forced the second

turn through sheer willpower. For a moment she thought she might land the jump too, but then her skate couldn't grab the ice. She fell with a thud that knocked the wind out of her and made her feel nauseous. No need to look up at the bleachers now, she knew the look that was on Mom's face.

KATHERINE COULDN'T believe it. Why the hell had Katie missed that jump? What did she think she was doing? This wasn't a game they were playing. Didn't she realize that?

KATIE WANTED TO beat at the ice with her fists and kick it with her skates. She wanted to scream so loud she drowned out Jiminy and Snow White and Ron and Mom. She wanted to cry. No more, she wanted to shout, no more jumps she couldn't make, no more skating when she was so scared she couldn't remember what she was doing, no more being a loser. She'd had it. She quit.

FOR A MOMENT SHE was afraid she had actually shouted the treacherous words out loud and she panicked. Then she realized she was still safe, and as always, the anger melted away. "I'm sorry," she whispered into the ice.

"Are you okay?" Ron asked as he skated over.

"Sure." She still felt sick from the fall and her body ached, but she stretched her lips into a game smile and started to get up.

"Want to take a minute to catch your breath?"

"I'm fine."

He held out his hand to help her but she scrambled to her feet without him. There were times when Ron was too nice to her. She would have felt better if he'd yelled at her. That was what she deserved.

"Okay," he said, "let's work on that toe loop."

She nodded. Ron skated over to turn off the recorder. She followed him. Inside her, the jumbled feelings had gone, leaving her hollow.

"We'll mark it slowly, starting with the approach," said Ron.

She took her position. The hollow feeling was growing; she tried to shake it off. Ron looked at her. "Hey, Katie, it was just a toe loop," he said gently. She tried to smile at him. But she had much bigger trouble than a missed jump. The warning signals were starting.

She told herself it wasn't happening. Even as her heart began to pound and she had to work for breath, she told herself it couldn't happen now.

"We have to analyze our problem and stay in control," Ron was saying.

Analyze. It was one of an athlete's strongest weapons. But how could she analyze when her heart was thumping so hard it was going to explode? How could she stay in control when she couldn't get enough air? Inside her, the fear mounted.

". . . distribution of weight," said Ron. It was a good sign that she could hear him, but she was getting light-headed. If she didn't do something fast, it would happen—the thing that must never happen when there were people around who might see. Her private craziness. She was going to space out. She pinched her arm, trying to dig her nails into her flesh to snap herself out of it. But the sleeve of her skating dress blocked the pain.

Ron was still talking, but now his words were too far away to hear. That meant it had started. Soon she'd feel as if she were disintegrating into hundreds of pieces, and she'd have no way to stop it. No power to stop the free fall of her mind that would end when it left her body. There was no other way to say it—that was what happened when she spaced out. Her mind left. She might go totally blank and afterward not be able to remember what she'd said or done. Or she might watch herself function from a long distance away. Either way, she'd be out of control. And scared. It was terrifying when her mind was gone and she couldn't think.

Later, when it was over, she'd want to cry and cry and never stop because it was humiliating to be so weak.

But there was a way to fight this loss of control. She knew how to take care of it, but she had to act fast, while she was still in charge.

"I've got to go to the locker room," she said in a voice that she could hear only as an echo. Through the distance she could see that Ron was surprised, but there was no time to worry about him. Everything in her was focused on what she had to do. She felt her legs propel her as she skated off the ice. Then, half wobbling, half running, she raced for the locker room.

WHEN SHE SAW Katie leave the ice, Katherine stormed down to the barricade and motioned Ron over. "What now?" she demanded.

"Katie broke a skate lace when she fell," he lied quickly. "She's in the locker room. Why don't you go back to your seat?"

He could tell she didn't trust him. "Don't worry," he said, "I'll make up the time she's missing without charging you. Just go sit."

She wasn't happy about it, but the lure of the extra time pacified her. She stomped back to her seat, leaving him to wonder what was really going on with Katie Roskova.

KATIE REACHED THE locker room and knelt on the floor next to her tote bag. It took only a second to find what she needed—a small pair of scissors wrapped in a square of soft cotton fabric. Originally the scissors were from a sewing kit her mom had given her in case she ever had to make emergency costume repairs, but Katie had found another use for them.

She pushed back the wrist-length sleeve of her skating dress and looked at the underside of her forearm, which was crisscrossed with dozens of small white and red scars. Quickly, she found a clear space near the elbow, and placed the blade of the scissors against the skin. Then, slowly and deliberately, she cut. The wound she made was really only a nick, but the pain she inflicted on herself steadied her. The wild, out-of-control feeling started to go away. The pain was doing its work. She repeated the movement again. This time the cut was longer and deeper. Blood came to the surface. The sight of the red drops on her skin calmed her even more. Her heart returned to its normal rhythm; she could breathe again. The blood held her gaze, the pain made her mind focus and kept it centered in her body. She knew she wasn't going to space out now. Relief flooded through her.

She dropped the scissors into her lap, leaned back against the wall of the locker room, and closed her eyes. The tensions of the morning seemed to drain away—all her doubts and fears were gone. She was completely relaxed now. The pain did that—it was like a medicine, at least when it was used properly, it was. She let her mind drift back to the first time she had discovered the healing power of pain. It had happened two years ago, when she was thirteen. She'd been alone in her bedroom; Katherine had just yelled at her for forgetting to iron her costume and had stormed off in a rage. And Katie had started to space out. Then suddenly she'd realized what she must do. It had come to her just like that. She had used a very special instrument that first time. Katie smiled as she remembered it. That was one of her best secrets.

She sat up and opened her eyes. Calmly she rewrapped the scissors and packed them away. This was all she used them for now, so they had to be treated very carefully. She checked her arm. The bleeding seemed to have stopped. She pulled her sleeve back down. Finally, she made her way from the locker room and out to the ice.

RON WAS STARTING to worry. He'd covered for Katie when she'd split because he figured the kid just needed a few minutes to pull herself together. But she'd been gone an awfully long time. If she'd really hurt herself when she had that spill . . . Before he could finish the thought, she reappeared in the arena.

"Okay, let's get on that jump," she said as she skated to him. Obviously, she wasn't going to explain her absence. But she was in good enough shape to work, and that was all he needed to know. With the championships less than six months away, they couldn't afford to lose valuable training time because Katie was nursing an injury.

After a few minutes, he realized that Katie was actually in very good shape. In fact, she was more relaxed and focused than she'd been all morning—possibly since they'd started preparing for the championships. By the end of the session she'd managed to do the double toe loop twice.

"Maybe you should fall more often," he kidded as they skated off the ice. For a second he thought she looked scared. Then she gave him a quick version of the lovely smile. "My best move," she said. "Should we work a couple more into the program?"

"Bite your tongue."

She smiled again and took off for the locker room to change. But as he watched her go he thought to himself that the fall really had helped. It happened that way with some kids—it was as if they could stop worrying once the worst had happened.

Katie's mother was coming toward him. From her expression something was displeasing her—the program probably. Or perhaps she thought Katie should have done a triple toe loop. He sighed. Stage mothers were an occupational hazard—probably a necessary evil—in his world, but that didn't mean he had to like them.

"Ms. Roskova," he said quickly before she could make her complaint, "there's something I want to talk to you about. Katie's going to have a lot of pressure in these next few months. We've got to try to keep her as relaxed as we can. If we can't do it ourselves, we may have to call in a sports shrink to help her."

As he'd figured it would, that idea stopped her cold. "Katie can handle a little pressure," she said tersely and walked away without another word.

But as he watched her go, it occurred to him that a psychologist for Katie might not be such a bad idea after all. Although he'd brought up the subject as a way of getting Katherine off his back, many athletes did, however, use therapists to help reduce stress. And Katie was going to have more stress than ever with the junior championships looming.

IN THE LOCKER room Katie changed quickly. She and Mom were always on a tight schedule in the mornings. It took a full hour to drive from the rink back to her school in New Rochelle and it was important that they make it in time for her second-period class. So far the school had been very understanding about Katie's skating schedule, allowing her to miss her first class so she could practice, but Mom didn't want to push their luck. Today, because Katie had taken time out, the session with Ron had run long. If she didn't hurry, they might be late. As she yanked off her skating dress she saw that the cut on her arm had opened again—probably because the sleeve of her skating dress was really tight around the elbow. From now on, she promised herself, she'd cut lower down. There were no Band-Aids in her tote, and she knew she couldn't ask her mom to stop and buy some without having to answer a lot of questions. So she blotted her arm with a tissue, and pulled on her long-sleeved blouse, which covered the wound. Before she went into school, she told herself, she'd have to remember to check to be sure the bleeding had stopped. Then she raced out to the parking lot where her mother was waiting in the car.

She expected her mom to be angry about the way she'd taken off during her lesson, but Katherine didn't mention it.

"I told you you could make that jump if you just tried," she said as Katie slid into the backseat of the car.

"I'm sorry," Katie said instantly, almost without thinking.

"What are you sorry for?"

Katie shrugged. "I don't know." She didn't want to explain

that the words had popped out because Katherine had seemed to be accusing her of not trying hard enough. A part of her wanted to scream that that wasn't fair. Another part of her was afraid it was true. And that made her feel guilty. Her mom worked so hard and sacrificed so much for the skating dream, and somehow Katie always felt she was failing her. She looked at Katherine sitting ramrod straight in the front seat as she drove the car. Her hair, as thick and black as Katie's, was pulled back in a dramatic bun, like a ballet dancer's. She was wearing a fitted red suit, with a red-and-black-striped blouse. Her mom dressed with much more style than the other women who worked at her bank. "I may have a loser's job, but I'm no frump," Katherine would say as she put on her stiletto high heels and outlined her lipsticked mouth with a pencil. In her mind Katie saw her mother's face, with the lines of anger that crossed her forehead and dug in deep on the sides of her nose. But there had been times when Katie had made her smile. She closed her eyes and remembered one of her favorites.

It had happened when she was eleven, on a cold evening in February. She'd qualified for her first big competition earlier in the day, and she could tell how excited her mom was. As they drove home from the rink, a light snow started to fall. By the time they reached their house, it was dark and the snow was several inches deep. Katherine turned into their driveway, but then instead of continuing into the garage she suddenly stopped and turned to Katie, saying, "Come on," getting out of the car and leaving the motor running and the lights on. Katie followed her. The beams from the headlights caught the falling snow, turning it into swirling flakes of glitter. Katherine laughed happily and pointed to the beam. "It's a spotlight, Katie," she said. "It's your spotlight."

And for once in her life Katie knew exactly what to do to make her mother happy. She raced into the center of the light and did a double pirouette. Then she threw her arms up in a grand gesture of triumph and dropped a curtsy in the snow. Katherine clapped her hands, and laughed, and ran into the light too. She grabbed Katie's hands and danced her around in a circle. Her mom's eyes were sparkling, her face was shiny. She was smiling a great big smile.

". . . HAVE YOU finished your homework?" Her mom's voice brought her back to the present. Katie opened her eyes and started working on her math.

SHE ALWAYS SPENT the trip back to New Rochelle doing whatever homework she hadn't been able to finish the night before. She went to a private school called the Westchester Academy, because a public school would have hassled them too much about all the time she took off for training and going to skating meets. Naturally they couldn't afford the tuition, so Katie was on full scholarship, which meant maintaining a B-plus average. Katie never went below an A minus.

She knew that as far as Mom was concerned, the whole school thing was nothing more than another obstacle they had to get around. If they'd had the money for a tutor, her mother would have dumped the academy long ago. Privately, Katie admitted to herself that she didn't mind school all that much. Sometimes studying seemed like a piece of cake— when you compared it with doing double toe loops. She opened her English book, and before long she was completely absorbed in her reading assignment.

By the time they reached the carved stone gates of the academy, she'd forgotten all about checking her arm to make sure it had stopped bleeding.

Katie lingered outside the front entrance of the school until she heard the bell ring for the end of the first period. Then she quickly slipped into the building and melted into the stream of students pouring into the hallway from the classrooms. Over the years she'd found that this was the best way to avoid attracting attention to her special schedule. She reversed the process at the end of each day when she left an hour early so she could go back to the rink for a second practice session. She wasn't sure why she tried so hard to keep a low profile at school—when she was younger she'd done it because she thought the other kids would like her more if she didn't seem too different. It was a plan that hadn't worked. No matter what she did she was different, and the other kids all knew it. Not that they were mean about it, she wasn't a geek after all, but she knew no one would ever think of her as a real friend.

She forced herself to slouch slightly—her high-energy skater's posture made her stand out too much—and she adopted the casual stroll of the other kids.

"Hey, Marie," she said as she passed a girl from her English class. "Hey, Grace, hi, Kimber." She made it a rule always to greet at least three people in the halls, and she always smiled confidently when she did it. She smiled a lot in school.

Katie picked up her pace so she was walking down the hall faster than the speed of traffic, and went back to her thoughts. Earlier in the year she'd thought she might have a real friend; there was a girl in her English class named Hilary who wrote beautiful poetry. Katie had complimented her on it after class and Hilary had told her how much she liked the funny story Katie had written about a cat who wanted to be a rock star. "I don't know where you get your crazy imagination," Hilary had said. Katie couldn't fathom how Hilary could write so intimately about her personal feelings. But she hadn't said that. For a few days they'd talked after class, but then Hilary had suggested that they get together for a movie at the mall on Saturday, and Katie had had to explain that on Saturdays she had a double practice session as well as a ballet class and tumbling. She'd said it as lightly as she could, as if it was no big deal, but she could see from the look on Hilary's face that she'd stopped being a potential friend and become "The Skater Who Was Different."

"It's just as well," said the voice in her head. "When you have girlfriends you have to tell each other all your secrets. What would you say when it was your turn? 'I've got this really gross thing I do to my arms'? That would make a big hit. You'd really be popular after that."

She knew she wouldn't tell deliberately. Nothing could ever make her blab her secrets to any friend, no matter how much she liked her. But there was always the possibility that she might let something slip if she let anyone get too close. So really, she was much safer the way she was.

Still, she couldn't help wondering what it would be like to have someone to talk to—about casual stuff like teachers, and clothes . . . and boys. Now there was a really scary thought—a boyfriend. She'd never even had a date. Mom would go ballistic if the subject ever came up.

"Hey, Katie," a girl named Tiffany said and gave her a little wave. Katie threw her a big, confident smile.

FINALLY SHE REACHED Ms. Moran's room, where she had her second-period English class. She hesitated for a moment, trying to decide whether to go in or to continue down the hallway on a mission that could be described only as a major geek move. Or, it would be if anyone realized what she was doing. With a pounding heart she passed the room and scurried down the hall as fast as she could without making a spectacle of herself. She kept going until she reached the farthest end of the building, opposite the entrance to the gym. There she backed into a corner, positioning herself so she could see everyone who passed, and waited. For a second she thought she was too late, but then a group of guys strolled past her on their way to the gym. Among them was Dave Malloy.

Dave was the last person anyone would have expected Katie Roskova to have a crush on. In fact, Katie wasn't sure that she did have a crush on him. He was older than she was—a senior—so they'd never really talked. More important, the word on Dave was that he was trouble. Everyone knew he would have been bounced from the academy if his very rich father hadn't bailed him out several times. But still, there was something about him that interested Katie. He had curly reddish blond hair and blue eyes, and he was muscular in a bulky kind of way which, she assumed, was fine for a football player. If he were a figure skater they'd make him trim down some. He wasn't the best-looking boy in school, but she liked the way he held himself when he walked. His attitude was kind of angry, as if he knew what people said about him and couldn't care less.

She had a daydream that one day they'd have a conversation and she'd tell him she understood how he felt because she was an outsider too. Maybe he'd want to get to know her then. "Right," said the voice inside her head. "And when he gets to know you, he'll find out how crazy you are. Then you can watch him run." The daydream died quickly. Katie knew in her heart that she was never going to have a boyfriend— or a best friend. She couldn't risk letting anyone get close enough to know her secrets. She sighed, shifted her book bag in her arms, and hurried back down the hall to Ms. Moran and her English class.

Katie liked English, and she liked Ms. Moran, who was young, and blonde, and had the kind of figure the boys made cracks about. Her first name was Jenny, and Katie thought she was a good teacher, even if she was a little soft on the kids who slacked off. Everyone knew you could get away with murder in her class if you could convince her that emotional problems were affecting your work. Ms. Moran was very big on working through your anxieties and depressions. Most of the time the kids didn't take advantage of her because they realized she was on their side. Besides, you could tell it really made her happy to give out good grades, and that seemed to make people work to get them. So maybe she was smart after all. Feminism was also very big with Ms. Moran. She was always going on about what an exciting time this was for young women because they could empower themselves. Whatever that meant.

Ms. Moran started the class that morning by handing back last week's essay assignment, which she'd just graded. As usual, she was going from desk to desk so she could tell each individual student what she liked about the work they'd done.

JENNY MORAN WORKED her way around her classroom giving out homework papers and compliments in equal measure. She knew there were times when she sounded like a Pollyanna, but she didn't care. She believed in the power of praise—both as a teaching tool and as a means of keeping the lines of communication open with her students. She wanted the kids to feel that they could trust her if they ever needed to talk.

One kid Jenny worried about was Katie Roskova. Not for any specific reason—the girl just seemed a little too good to be true. Maybe it's just that I'm such a couch potato myself, Jenny thought, so I don't understand the kind of drive an athlete like Katie has. Or maybe she'd read too many articles about overstressed female figure skaters and gymnasts. All she knew was, she was suspicious about any system in which adults drove young kids to win at any cost. And there was something about Katie's never-ending discipline that was unnerving. If every once in a while she'd miss a homework assignment, I'd feel better about her, Jenny thought. As for Katie's perpetual poise and good humor, Jenny thought even bad moods and temper tantrums would be preferable—anything but the too big smile the kid constantly wore. She was wearing it now as she waited for Jenny to approach her desk.

Jenny pulled Katie's paper out of the stack she was carrying. "Nice work, Katie," said Jenny. "I like your insights into the contrast between Dorothy Parker's private life and her public persona." She held out the paper, and Katie reached up to take it.

LATER ON, WHEN she was piecing it all together, Katie would realize that that was the moment that started everything. At the time, all she knew was that when she lifted her arm to take her homework assignment from Ms. Moran, she saw blood on her sleeve. It wasn't a little speck—that had happened once or twice before and no one had noticed—no, this was a big, oval-shaped blotch. It was still wet, and very red. Obviously her wound had reopened all the way. Maybe it was carrying the book bag that had done it. She stared at the stain in horror, then quickly tried to pull her arm back so Ms. Moran wouldn't see. But she wasn't fast enough.

"Katie, is your arm bleeding?" asked Ms. Moran. "Have you hurt yourself?"

Katie couldn't think of an answer. Her mind was too busy

protesting that this was not supposed to happen. Her blood was supposed to be private. She used it when she needed it and kept the need in a separate compartment, away from the rest of her life. All of her secrets were in compartments; that was how she lived. If the walls of those compartments started to come down, everything would get all jumbled up together and she would lose control. That would be terrifying. It would be chaos . . .

". . . if you'd like, Katie?" Ms. Moran was still talking; obviously she was asking about the cut. Katie made herself concentrate. There was still time to get the walls back in place if she could just think fast enough.

"I'm not sure," she said carefully, hoping that covered whatever Ms. Moran had been going on about.

"I really do think the nurse should have a look at your arm," said Ms. Moran.

And while she was looking, the nurse would see all of Katie's scars. "Think of something to say," screamed the voice in her head. "Get the walls back up."

"It's just a scrape," she said to Ms. Moran. "I fell this morning when I was practicing. It's no big deal."

"Still—" Ms. Moran began, but Katie cut her off.

"I'll go see the nurse right after class," she said reassuringly. Ms. Moran was still holding out the homework assignment. Katie smiled and made herself reach out for it. But her face felt so stiff she couldn't manage more than a weak grin. She was careful to use the arm that wasn't cut.

As JENNY HANDED the paper to Katie, she wondered what was going on with the girl. Her explanation of the skating fall made perfect sense. So why did she seem so afraid? Or was she? Was it just Jenny's imagination? One thing Jenny was sure of, Katie had no intention of going to the nurse. Again, why? Did she see it as a sign of weakness? Was she ashamed to admit she'd hurt herself? Jenny sighed. All of her suspicions about bullying coaches and driven parents came back to haunt her. But there was nothing she could do to help. Jenny sighed again and went on to the next student.

— ❋ —

KATIE HELD HER breath until Ms. Moran walked away from her desk. After the teacher was gone, she sat frozen in her seat, unable to move.

"Way to go, stupid," she raged at herself silently. "You knew that arm was bleeding, why didn't you go to the bathroom and fix it? What are you trying to do? Let everyone know what a whacked-out nutcase you really are? Why don't you just wear a neon sign over your head?" And as she sat erect and unseeing, the panic flooded back into her as strong as it had been when she was on the ice trying to do a double toe loop. But now it was even worse. Because now the fear was centered on a person—Ms. Moran.

Ms. Moran wasn't like the other teachers. Ms. Moran noticed things. And she was thoughtful. What if, when she was thinking it over, she realized that Katie was lying about the blood on her sleeve? What if, somehow, some way, Ms. Moran managed to figure out what Katie had done? That was the nightmare—that someday someone would find out. The compartments would be smashed and the secrets would be out where everyone could see them. And no one would understand. Not even someone as kind as Ms. Moran. Katie slumped in her seat. Sometimes she got so tired. Sometimes she thought it would be a relief to tell someone. Maybe someone who was kind and nice like Ms. Moran . . . She pulled herself up abruptly. That was what made Ms. Moran so dangerous. It wasn't just that she noticed things, there was something about her that made you want to tell her things—things that must never, ever be told. From now on, Katie decided, she was going to be very careful around Ms. Moran.

But Katie soon realized that it wasn't just Ms. Moran she had to guard against. She tried to push the incident in English class out of her mind, but it stayed with her for the rest of the day. She couldn't stop wondering what it would be like if she got caught. Every time she talked to someone, the voice inside her head asked the person, "What would you do if I showed you the scars on my arm? What would you do if I told you how I got them?"

It wasn't until she got home that night that she realized how dangerous that kind of thinking could be. She and her mom sat in the dining alcove, which was really just a part of the kitchen because the house was too small to have a real dining room. Mom hated their house because it was cheap and looked like all the others on their cul-de-sac.

"This is your father's lousy taste, he picked this hole," Katherine was fond of saying. Then she'd add, "And he stuck me with the damn mortgage." She and Katie's dad had bought the house two years before they divorced. According to the settlement, her father was supposed to help with the mortgage payments, but somehow he never seemed to get around to it. But then he never got around to visiting his only daughter either. He lived out of state and it had been months since Katie had last seen him. Katherine told her she didn't need her father and that she was better off without him. Katie was inclined to agree.

Usually Katherine ate in silence, too tired and angry from her day to talk, but tonight she was in a good mood. "Someday we'll get out of this dump," she said as she speared a piece of the frozen potpie Katie had microwaved. "You've got the double toe loop now. If you work the way you did this morning, you'll be doing a triple before the competition. I keep telling you it's all in your attitude—just stop making such a fuss about those jumps and go out and do them . . ."

For some reason her mother's good humor made Katie angry. The question she'd been tossing at everyone in her mind that day came back in full force. "I wonder what you'd do if I showed you what I did in the locker room before the double toe loop, Mom," said the voice in her head. "I wonder how happy you'd be about my attitude then." What she said out loud was, "Could I have the salt?" Then she did something weird. Or at least, a part of her did it. Slowly and deliberately, she reached across her mother for the saltshaker—almost shoving her sleeve with the dried bloodstain in front of Katherine's eyes. A portion of her mind watched, horrified, as her arm made the move, but there was nothing she could do to stop herself. "See the blood, Mom," the voice inside her head commanded her mother. "See it and ask me what happened. 'Cause I'll tell you. I'll show you my scars, and I'll describe how I got every single one of them. I'll give you all the details." But even while those words were going through her head, another voice in her brain was yelling at her to get her arm out of there fast. This was dangerous, it screamed. Katherine must not discover the secrets. Katie couldn't even imagine how awful it would be if she did.

The second voice finally won and she was at last able to pull back her arm. She sat, motionless, holding her breath, waiting for her mother to start asking about the bloodstain. Her heart pounded so loudly she could hear it as she braced herself for the inevitable attack.

But the only thing that happened was that her mother handed her the saltshaker. "You use too much of that stuff," she said. "You don't want to retain water."

Katie took the shaker with a trembling hand and forced herself to breathe. Katherine had been so absorbed in her dreams for the future she hadn't even noticed the bloodstain thrust in front of her eyes. Relief flooded through Katie. I'll never do anything that stupid again, she promised herself.

After dinner she locked the bathroom door, took off her blouse, and washed out the blood by hand before sticking it in the washer with her other clothes. Since she did her own laundry, it really wasn't necessary. But from now on, she promised herself, she was going to be extra careful.

But in the days that followed, Katie wasn't careful. In fact, she suddenly seemed to get extremely careless about covering her tracks. It was as though almost getting caught had started her on a roller-coaster ride she couldn't stop. She also seemed to be spacing out more, and just about anything could start it.

Two weeks after her near miss in Ms. Moran's class, she stood outside the school cafeteria waiting to join the lunch line. She was always careful to wait until the end so she could see where everyone else was sitting and join a couple of kids she knew. She never took a chance on sitting first and waiting for someone to join her. Lunch was a heavily social time and the kids tended to separate into their tribes. An outsider like Katie could find herself eating in miserable solitude if she didn't plan carefully. But on this day she was in luck; she spotted Hilary sitting with two other girls at a table with three empty seats left. Perfect. She grabbed her nonfat yogurt, salad, and extra fruit for energy during her afternoon skating session, and headed for Hilary and her friends.

At the table she did the body language that asked the wordless question "Can I sit?" got a similarly expressed permission, and slid into a chair quietly without interrupting the conversation.

". . . because he is way cute," a girl named Margie Berman was saying.

"I liked him better before he started wearing that dorky goatee," said a brunette who was called Dru by the people who knew her well. "And anyway, the real babe on the show is his brother."

Obviously they were talking about some actor on television. Since Katie seldom had time to watch TV, she settled in to listen, nod, make noncommittal noises, and be bored. Instead, Hilary turned to her.

"Katie, I'm having a party at my house on Friday night," she said. "Want to come?"

"It's really just a big excuse for Hil to get to dance with Ted McKee," giggled Margie. "She's got the hots for him—"

"I do not," Hilary said, blushing scarlet and punching her. But she was laughing too.

"Ted is a major babe," said Dru, and she joined in the giggles. Katie watched the three of them and felt something sad twist inside her.

"So can you come, Katie?" asked Hilary.

It would be against the rules. She had to be in bed by ten every night, so she could get her rest. Katherine would never allow it. The only answer was no.

But she wanted to say yes so much. She wanted to giggle and blush and ask Hilary if she'd mind inviting David Malloy to the party. And Hilary would say yes because she wanted to be Katie's friend, and Dru and Margie would tease her. And if Dave did go, maybe they could dance together . . .

"Stupid," jeered the voice in her head. "You don't know how to dance the way these kids do. You do ballet. You do toe loops and camel spins. You've never danced with a boy in your life. You'd make a total fool of yourself."

The other three girls were waiting for her to accept the invitation.

"I can't stay out late," she said softly.

"Not even on Friday night?" demanded Dru.

"It's just . . . I have to get up so early on Saturday." There was a tone in her voice that was pleading with them to understand. She hated hearing herself beg. And she hated them for making her feel that she had to.

"But Saturday's the weekend," Margie protested. "Everyone sleeps in on Saturday."

"Katie has to skate and stuff on Saturday," Hilary explained in a way that seemed kind, but Katie knew it was full of pity.

She wanted to slap them all across their silly faces. "Don't you dare feel sorry for me," she wanted to shout. "I'm going to be a star and you'll be nothing."

But then suddenly, the sounds in the cafeteria began to echo ominously. Margie said, "Bummer," and Katie listened as the word bounced off the walls . . . And she knew she was in trouble . . .

She made the corners of her mouth turn up in a smile. "It is a bummer," she heard herself agree in a voice that was coming from much too far away. "But I get to work out with this real cool guy . . ." The girls perked up immediately—they were too stupid to know that as a solo performer she never practiced with anyone. Dru was going to ask for details, she could tell, so she added quickly, "He looks a lot like Brian Boitano did, back when he won the gold in Calgary." Since none of them had a clue as to who Boitano was, it shut them up. But she still had to find an excuse to get out of there—and she had to do it fast. She looked around desperately. Her yogurt was sitting on the table in front of her. She reached out with hands she could barely control and opened it. Her breathing was starting to get ragged. "Oh, yuk," she gasped, "there's a bug in this; I've got to get a new one." And before anyone could stop her, she stood up, grabbed her stuff, and left the table.

She walked to the girls' room as fast as she could without attracting attention. Once there, she found an empty stall, pulled out her scissors, and did what had to be done.

AFTER IT WAS over, she put the scissors away and went back out into the hallway. She'd cut herself many times before at school, so everything should have been okay.

But it wasn't. Because for some reason, she forgot that her next class was world history. Her mind was playing tricks on her, she later realized, and that was what was so scary. So instead of going to world history, she walked to Ms. Moran's classroom in a kind of fog. She was standing outside the door, about to go in, when she was jolted by a voice at her side.

"Katie, are you okay?" asked a girl she knew vaguely—Susan Something.

The fog cleared abruptly. Katie forced herself to laugh. "I must have been daydreaming, and came here by mistake," she said, making a comical face. "Can you believe what a total spaz I am?"

"I meant—what's wrong with your arm?" asked Susan.

And that was when Katie saw the blood smeared up and down the length of her sleeve. The stains were dramatic: This was not the result of a little blood accidentally seeping from a cut. This had been done deliberately. It was almost like showing off. And the worst of it was, she couldn't remember doing it.

Susan was looking at her curiously.

Katie made herself take a deep breath. "Don't explain too much," the voice in her head warned.

"Boy, I really racked myself up," she said cheerfully. "Guess I better get a couple of Band-Aids." And she walked off.

After she got halfway down the hall she ran for her locker, grabbed her skating sweater, and raced into the girls' room to change in the stall.

"Stupid, stupid, stupid!" yelled the voice in her head as she undid her buttons with shaking hands.

But I did get away with it, a part of her mind thought.

7

Three days after she had almost barged into Ms. Moran's room at the wrong time, Katie slipped up again and walked into the English teacher's class with blood on her sleeve. This time it wasn't anything spectacular, but the stain was big enough for Ms. Moran to see and mention. Then a few days later, it happened again.

Both times she'd known her arm was still bleeding when she'd put on her blouse. Both times she'd reminded herself to check her sleeve before she walked into Ms. Moran's classroom. And both times she'd forgotten—the same way she'd forgotten she was supposed to be going to world history instead of English. That was what was so terrifying. She could control what she thought and did and said, but how could she control what she forgot?

WHEN THE SECOND slipup happened, Ms. Moran picked up on it just as class was ending. Katie tried to get out of the room, but Ms. Moran stopped her.

"I've got a free period," she said in that super laid-back tone adults always used when they wanted to put a kid at ease. "Why don't you hang out a little?"

"I have a class," Katie said.

"I'll give you a pass. This won't take long. I just wanted to say that I'm a little concerned. It seems to me that you've been getting hurt a lot lately. Are you okay?"

"It's no big deal," Katie said quickly. "I've been skating kind of hard, that's all." She did a little shrug to show how unimportant it was. Meanwhile, the voice inside her head yelled, "Leave me alone."

Ms. Moran smiled. "I know you haven't gone to the nurse," she said mildly. "I'm not going to lecture you because you're smart enough to realize that you could get an infection if you don't take care. It does bother me that you seem to keep reinjuring that same arm in the same area. Maybe you need some stitches."

"Oh, I can explain that," Katie said quickly. Did she sound too eager? It was so hard to get it right. "I'm working on this one step in my skating program . . . it's a jump actually . . ." Stick with the truth whenever you could, she thought. It helped when you were lying. ". . . and each time I fall at the same point, so I land the same way. I guess that's why I keep scraping my arm in the same place." She wanted to look at Ms. Moran's face to see if she was buying it, but she forced herself not to. "Why can't you just leave me alone?" the voice in her head demanded.

"You'll have to forgive me," said Ms. Moran. "I'm a real wimp when it comes to pain. All that falling must hurt a lot," she added gently.

It was the gentleness that did it. Without meaning to, Katie heard herself say in a soft voice, "Sometimes you have to get hurt. It's the only way . . ."

She saw how carefully Ms. Moran was listening.

"Stupid, you're letting her get to you," said the voice in her head. "Why don't you just roll up your sleeve and show her your scars?" She covered quickly with a grin. "What I meant was, you know what they say, 'No pain, no gain.' "

"Katie, there's a difference—" Ms. Moran began, but Katie cut her off.

"Can I tell you something that makes me kind of mad?" she asked, giving the woman her most eager look.

Ms. Moran nodded—naturally.

Katie drew a deep breath. "If I were a guy on one of the teams, no one would say anything if I got a little banged up every once in a while. Look at the football players—they're always spraining something," she said and smiled. Ms.

Moran smiled with her. So far, so good. Katie leaned in. "The thing is," she said earnestly, "I'm an athlete too. Even if I am just a girl, and even if my sport is figure skating. Sometimes I fall or I pull a muscle, the same way the boys do. And I can take it—like the boys. I just wish people respected that." She sat back triumphantly. No way the great feminist could argue with that.

"I see your point, Katie," said Ms. Moran slowly. "I hadn't thought of it as a question of respect. Thank you for educating me." She really was awfully nice. Katie had a moment of regret. Then she told herself not to be crazy.

Ms. Moran went to her desk. "You'll be late for your next class," she said. "Let me make out that pass."

Katie watched her with a feeling of deep relief. The danger was past. She'd won. She swore to herself that she would never, ever let herself get into another of these little "talks" with Ms. Moran.

AFTER KATIE WAS gone, Jenny sat at her desk thinking about her. Jenny had taught her share of athletes, both male and female, but she'd never seen any kid ignore injuries the way Katie seemed to. Even if she was trying to prove she could out-tough the boys, there were limits. Plus, the girl did seem to be awfully accident-prone. She got up and headed for the door. Maybe she'd pay a visit to the nurse's office. This was one of the two days a week when Ilene Santiago, the school psychologist, was in.

8

"Jenny, give me a break," said Ilene. She was sitting at her desk in the office she shared with the school's nurse, Barbara Quinn. Barbara, who was at her desk, looked up from some paperwork.

"If you want me to make myself scarce, Ilene, I can go to the teachers' lounge," she offered.

"I'd like you to listen too," said Jenny.

Barbara was a big, earthy woman in her mid-fifties. Jenny didn't know her very well, but she was extremely popular with the kids.

"Sure, if I can help," said Barbara.

"Jenny, let me tell you what's going on here, from my point of view," said Ilene. She brushed a stray wisp of her otherwise perfectly coiffed hair from her face with an exquisitely manicured right hand. Jenny had always been a little in awe of the way the psychologist turned herself out.

"We've got three girls in this school who are anorexics bent on starving themselves to death," said Ilene. "We've got at least two kids who should be in rehab for illegal substances, but Mommy and Daddy are in such deep denial we'll probably have to wait until we're actually looking at an overdose before anything can be done. Don't get me started on the kids who are drinking too much and having unsafe sex. Now, we're facing all of this, and you want me to evaluate a girl whose only problem is she's falling down too much because she's training to be an Olympic athlete? Let's not forget, this is also a kid who is maintaining an A-minus average."

Jenny felt herself flush. "I didn't say I wanted you to do an evaluation on her. I just thought the two of you could have a talk."

"My role here in this school is not to practice therapy."

"I know, but you do monitor kids who are in trouble, don't you?" asked Jenny, feeling dumber by the minute. She realized she really didn't know what Ilene did—in her three years as a teacher at the school she'd never sent a student to the psychologist.

"Only if that 'trouble' interferes with their ability to function in school. I step in when the academic performance is suffering. Then, if it's appropriate, I'll refer the kid to a therapist. But only then."

"So if a kid's hanging off the rafters at home you can't do anything as long as she's getting passing grades?"

"Not unless she's acting out here in school in ways that are disruptive to the rest of the students. Which this girl is not."

"No, she isn't," Jenny admitted. "But that's not the point . . ." Suddenly she was feeling incompetent and a little ridiculous. She had the feeling Ilene made most people feel that way.

"So what's bothering you?" asked Barbara.

"In the past two weeks she's come into my class bleeding on four separate occasions. She says it's because she's training hard."

"Do you believe her?" asked Barbara.

"I don't know . . . Yes, I guess so . . . I mean, there's no reason not to . . ." said Jenny. "But it's not just the injuries, it's her attitude toward them that disturbs me. She ignores them; she seems to feel she's got to suffer in silence."

"She's going after a goal; she doesn't have time to nurse every little ache and pain," said Ilene.

"But she could take two minutes to see me for a Band-Aid," offered Barbara. She looked at Jenny thoughtfully. "I wonder why she doesn't."

"Because she doesn't like the nurse's office. Or she doesn't like Band-Aids. Will you listen to yourselves? This is a teenager we're talking about. Explain why they do half the things they do," said Ilene.

"But Katie's not leading a normal teenager's life," said Barbara.

"What's normal for kids these days?" asked Ilene.

"Have you ever heard the girl laugh?" Jenny demanded. "I'm not talking about that slick professional smile she pulls when adults are around . . . I mean a real kid's laugh. Who are her friends? What does she do for fun?"

Ilene sighed. "If you're asking if Katie's under too much pressure, the answer is probably—yes, from time to time she is. But it's up to her mother to watch out for that."

"What if the mother is part of the problem? I've read about the coaches and parents of young girls who compete in sports on Katie's level. Some of the stories are horrendous."

"Those are the ones that make the news." Ilene made a steeple out of her scarlet fingernails and contemplated it. "Look, not every kid who excels at something winds up psychologically damaged. Some overachievers are actually very happy, and competition doesn't necessarily kill—contrary to popular mythology. So what if Katie has to make some sacrifices in order to be the best in her sport? So what if every once in a while too much is asked of her? Trust me, she's better off than most kids who are never challenged enough. All things considered, Katie's one of the luckiest young girls I know."

And that, Jenny knew, was the party line on Katie Roskova at Westchester Academy. The school had great respect for kids who were goal oriented. Bright, pretty, talented Katie was one of its golden girls.

Ilene stood up to usher her out. Jenny shot a look at Barbara, who shrugged and sighed.

"If she's not asking for help . . . ," she said, her voice trailing off.

"I know. And it's probably nothing," said Jenny.

"Probably," said Barbara.

"I promise you, there's nothing wrong with that kid," said Ilene firmly.

9

Katie's triumph over Ms. Moran was short-lived. That after-noon she had the worst practice session she'd had in months. Forget a triple toe loop, or even a double, she fell landing a single. Even her spins were rocky. Her mom's lips got tighter and tighter as Ron looked more and more wor-ried. Finally, he ended the session early and sent Katie off to the locker room to change. As she left the rink she saw Ron signal Katherine in the bleachers—obviously he was calling an emergency conference. Normally it was her mom who initiated these little summit meetings. Katie stayed as far away from them as she could because the main event usually included raking poor Ron over the coals. But this time was different. Katie wondered what Ron wanted to talk about. As she headed for the locker room she saw him start speaking, leaning forward earnestly, his breath coming out in little frozen puffs. Mom did not look happy.

Fifteen minutes later, when Katie came back from chang-ing, they were sitting in the row of seats near the arena entrance, still talking. In fact, they were so absorbed in their conversation they didn't notice her come up behind them. A little wall blocked the entrance from the view of the seats. It took Katie about two seconds to decide to duck behind the wall so she could eavesdrop.

". . . it happens sometimes after a girl hits puberty," Ron was saying. "Some kids just can't adapt to all the changes their bodies go through."

"That's ridiculous," said Katherine. "Katie's gained exactly ten pounds since she turned thirteen, and she's only grown an inch and a half."

"But her weight keeps redistributing itself as she develops . . ."

"Girls cope with that," her mom snapped. "Developing breasts didn't hurt Yamaguchi or Kerrigan. And Katie isn't even very big, thank God."

Katie felt her face go red. For a moment she wondered how she'd ever be able to face Ron again. "Don't be stupid," jeered the voice inside her head. Her body was her instrument; of course Ron monitored the changes that were going on with it—that was his job. But still, she felt embarrassed. The whole puberty thing made her feel weird . . . and kind of messy somehow.

HER MOM HAD made it clear how she felt about the process. When Katie was around eleven, she'd been curious and a little excited about the prospect of getting her period. Katherine had very quickly let her know that it was nothing more than a potential impediment to their main goal. "I don't want to hear a lot of garbage about cramps or not being able to work out," she'd said firmly. "When you start menstruating you just ignore it and you won't even notice it's happening."

So on the morning when Katie had her first period, her mom had calmly handed her a Kotex pad and two pairs of underpants. "Put these on under your tights," she'd said.

"Shouldn't I wear slacks?" Katie had asked hesitantly.

"Don't be ridiculous. Put on your pink skating skirt the way you planned."

The pink skirt barely covered her ruffled panties.

"But what if someone sees . . ." Katie began.

"Katie, I'm not going to let you indulge yourself in a lot of hysteria over nothing."

She'd worn the skirt, and prayed that no one would see the bulge between her legs when she jumped and spun—and fell.

And her mom had been right—no one had noticed. But it had been the longest practice session of Katie's life.

"See?" said Katherine when the endless hour finally came to a close. "There's no problem with this unless you make it one. And you'll never be sick either. I've never had a single cramp. It's mind over matter."

Mind over matter was her mom's favorite saying. She was using it now.

"It's mind over matter, Ron. Katie will just have to work a little harder." She said it in the tone that was a warning that this conversation was now over. But for once Ron ignored her. "It's not always that easy," he persisted. "In addition to the more visible changes, Katie's dealing with fluctuations in muscle strength and energy. What you've got to understand is, every few months she's skating with what is essentially a brand-new body."

Katie knew exactly what he was talking about. In the past two years it had felt as if her body was playing tricks on her because of the way it kept changing. And it did make her skating more difficult—especially in the jumps, where anything could throw her off. She'd never really thought about it before, but suddenly it seemed unfair that this was happening to her. She had enough problems without being betrayed by her own changing body. She was starting to get mad about it, but then she heard Ron say to her mother, "Sometimes it gets to be too much for a kid. I don't believe in kids competing when it's no longer fun, Ms. Roskova. I mean . . ." He sounded awkward. "I think Katie should at least have the option of deciding if she wants to go on . . ."

Katie leaned against the wall, her anger turning to panic in an instant. Quit? The idea was impossible. She'd been on the ice for as long as she could remember. She slid down the glazed brick of the entryway until she was sitting on the wet rubber flooring of the arena. She couldn't imagine life without practice sessions and lessons. More important, she couldn't imagine how she'd live without something important to shoot for. Her life was focused on being an Olympic skater. How did other people live without a goal like that? How did they feel worthwhile? She pulled herself back up to listen again.

". . . crazy, stupid, dumb things I've ever heard in my life," her mom was raging. "We'll work harder. We'll be fine. We are not going to quit."

For once her mother's anger was comforting to hear. Mom was right. She'd have to work harder. She'd beat this body that was betraying her. She'd beat the new, soft, lumpy mess it was becoming. It wasn't going to stop her.

THE TALK WITH Ron had made her mom mad. They drove home from the rink in a dark and angry silence. Katie tried to concentrate on her science homework, but a part of her was waiting for the explosion that she knew would come sooner or later. When her mother was this angry, there was always an explosion—the only question was what would trigger it.

IT WAS ALMOST seven by the time they got home. Katie still had her English assignment to finish in addition to ironing her school clothes for the next day. She opened up her books and went to work at the kitchen table. Ms. Moran had let them choose the subjects for their American literature term papers and Katie had gone with her beloved Dorothy Parker.

> *Oh life is a glorious cycle of song,*
> *A medley of extemporania.*
> *And love is a thing that can never go wrong*
> *And I am Marie of Rumania.*

It was the kind of humor Katie loved—the last line was a quiet little zinger said under the breath. Dorothy had once said, "A girl's best friend is her mutter." Katie giggled softly. Unfortunately, it wasn't too soft for Katherine to hear as she was washing up the dishes. And that one soft giggle was all it took.

"This is the problem," Katherine shouted as she tossed the dishcloth into the sink and strode over to Katie. "You and your goddamn books. If you'd spend as much energy on your skating as you do on these, you'd have an easy triple toe loop."

Katie knew she should sit quietly and tune out the tirade as much as she could. It was what she usually did. Eventually the storm would pass. But that night she wanted to defend herself. She looked down at the book in her lap so she wouldn't meet her mother's eyes. "I have to keep up my grade average, to hang on to my scholarship," she said softly. Needless to say, it was a big mistake.

"Don't give me that. You love all that stuff. Reading those books for your English teacher and wasting your time writing extra reports for her. Don't think I don't know. Well, what is it going to get you? What kind of life does your precious Ms. Moran have on her lousy salary? She kills herself all day long trying to teach a bunch of snotty rich kids who could care less. And their snotty rich parents treat her like something you could scrape off the bottom of your shoe. Is that what you want? Is it?" Katherine's voice was getting higher and higher. She reached into Katie's lap and grabbed the book of Dorothy Parker's poems. "Is this crap what you want for the rest of your life?" she yelled as she threw the book at the kitchen counter. It hit a glass, which fell to the floor and shattered. For a second both Katie and Katherine stared at the glittering pieces on the immaculate kitchen floor.

"Sometimes you're so stupid," Katherine hissed in the suddenly silent kitchen. "Clean up that mess. I'm going to bed." And she walked out.

For a long time Katie sat still, staring at the broken shards of glass on the floor. Finally, she got up and began sweeping. One piece of glass was shaped like a triangle. Katie picked it up and held it in her hand, watching it reflect the light. Then she slipped it into her pocket and dumped the rest into the trash. She left her books still open on the kitchen table and went into the bathroom. It was funny, she thought, how little she felt. There was no frantic loss of control, no spacing out. It was almost as if she'd been programmed.

In the bathroom she locked the door. If Katherine wanted to come in, she'd have to break it down. Which actually might be kind of fun to watch. Katie gave herself a few seconds to enjoy the fantasy of Katherine banging on the door until the skin on her knuckles broke and her hands started to bleed. "How much mind over matter will you have when you're looking at your own blood, Mom?" asked the voice inside her head. "I can do it, I'm tough enough. How about you? Can you do what I do?"

She took the glass shard out of her sweater pocket and placed it on the sink. Then she pulled off the cardigan, folded it neatly, and draped it over the side of the tub. Her blouse followed. She was down to her bra now. She'd started wearing one only a year ago. She reached back to unhook it and shrugged it off.

Her breasts were small, as her mom had said. In the mirror they seemed whiter than her face. She'd never looked at them much; it was almost as if by ignoring them she could make them go away. They were a part of her problem, the part of the body betrayer that changed and fluctuated and made life so difficult. But now she was going to look at them very carefully. She picked up the glass shard and ran her finger lightly over the edge. It was sharp enough. It would cut. She held it firmly.

She felt exhilarated, and a little breathless, as if she'd been skating her long program double-time. In the mirror her eyes sparkled back. "This one's for me," said the voice in her head. She began her examination of the two small mounds on her chest.

They had a soft, round look; the nipples were pale pink circles—except at the very center. She shifted the glass shard from her right hand to her left. Then, with her right forefinger she traced a circle around the left breast. The skin felt silky, and it was so thin she could see a cross-hatching of blue veins right under the surface. For a moment that stopped her; those prominent veins were a little scary. She put down the glass shard with its sharp cutting edge. But as soon as she did it, she felt disappointed—so disappointed she was afraid she'd start screaming and hitting the tile walls with her fists. She wanted to use the piece of glass. There were so many things she wasn't allowed to do. This one was for her. She had earned it. Quickly she picked up the shard again, this time in her right hand, and reached across to her left breast. But once again the veins stopped her. There seemed to be more of them near the nipple—that was where they connected with one another like blue roads on a map. Her hand hovered over them, but in the end she decided to play it safe.

She picked a spot at the top of the breast almost at her armpit. In the mirror she watched as her hand pushed the sharp point of the glass shard into the soft, white skin until it broke. She let the red blood come to the surface around the piece of glass, then with one quick, firm stroke she made her cut. "Mind over matter, Mom," said the voice in her head. "Mind over matter." Then she sat on the floor and waited. The familiar, welcome feeling of relief and well-being was immediate. She leaned back against the side of the tub and floated.

But not for long. Because fear began creeping back into her mind. She tried to push it back, to regain her sense of peace, but the fear persisted. What she had done was wrong, it said. Ever since she'd discovered the power of pain and blood she had treated them carefully, with great respect. They were her medicine; she used them only when she was spacing out. But this time she'd cut for different reasons. There had been no danger of spacing out, she'd done it just because she'd wanted to. Now thoroughly frightened, she sat upright. In some way she couldn't define, she'd broken the rules. And breaking the rules always led to trouble.

She felt her wound start to throb. But there was no comfort in it. Suddenly she was overcome with a need to clean up. She scrambled to her feet.

There was more blood than usual, maybe because the shard of glass wasn't as sharp as her scissors, so she'd had to cut deeper. Or maybe it was because it was her breast. She didn't know, she was just aware of an overpowering need to get rid of all evidence of what she'd done. Several drops of blood had fallen on the floor. She got down on her knees and began mopping them up with a towel. She was particularly careful with one spot that had fallen on the grouting between two tiles, rubbing and scrubbing it until there was no trace of telltale pink left. Finally, she was satisfied that no sign of what had happened remained. She stood up and rinsed the towel first in cold water and then in hot. Later she would sneak it into her laundry and wash it with her clothes. It didn't matter that her mother would never notice a reddish stain on a towel, or ask about it. Katherine wasn't the one she was cleaning up for. Or trying to hide from.

She found a Band-Aid in the medicine cabinet and covered her cut. She rarely put Band-Aids on her arm, especially when she cut herself at home, but this was different. This wound must be covered.

LATER AS SHE lay in bed trying to sleep, another even more frightening thought occurred to her. What if, by breaking the rules, she'd somehow taken away the power of her medicine? What if the next time she needed it to keep herself from spacing out, it didn't work because she'd abused it? She wasn't sure exactly why she was so afraid this had happened, it was just an instinct that told her it could have. She sat upright. She had to know. She had to find out before morning, when she would have to go to the rink, and school, and all the other dangerously public places where a disaster could occur if she no longer had a way to stop it.

There was only one way to check. She had to have a test. Which meant somehow she had to force herself to space out so she could try to stop it. But how could she do that? Spacing out was a random thing; she never knew when it was going to happen, or why. So how could she bring it on at will? She closed her eyes and tried to force herself to remember how it felt when the warning signs began. She managed to dredge up a recollection of being light-headed, with a heart that was racing so fast it felt like it would burst. But it was as if she'd never experienced it personally. It could have been something she'd read about in a book. She tried to make herself dizzy by breathing too fast and shallow but her body refused to cooperate and took in only as much oxygen as it needed. Finally, she gave up.

For a long time she lay in bed, afraid. But then the discipline of a lifetime kicked in, and she forced herself to drift off into a troubled sleep.

THE NEXT MORNING she was scared enough to consider trying to fake being sick. But she knew she'd have to be at death's door before her mom would let her miss a day of practice. As she got dressed she carefully avoided looking at the hateful new wound that had caused all her trouble. Then before she went into the kitchen to face Katherine she double-checked to be sure her scissors were wrapped and in her bag. "Please let it still work," she prayed to herself.

But it seemed that her late-night terror was for nothing. Because she didn't space out that day, or the day after, or the day after that. Finally, a full week had gone by without an incident. At first she couldn't believe it. But she counted up the days on the kitchen calendar and it was true. She tried to remember the last time she'd gone this long, and drew a blank.

For a while the apparent miracle made her happy. She even let herself hope that it was over—maybe the spacing out had suddenly stopped. It was possible. That was the way it had started—abruptly, and without warning. But she didn't really believe her nightmare had ended. And with each day that it didn't happen she got more afraid that when it did she wouldn't be able to control it.

"Jerk," said the voice inside her head. "You stupid, stupid jerk. What are you going to do now?"

THE FIRST WEEK stretched into a second and a third and nothing happened. Except that she got more nervous and restless. For some reason, the worst place for her seemed to be school. Sitting still in a classroom for forty-five minutes became torture. Trying to absorb what a teacher was saying seemed impossible. For the first time in her life reading a book felt like a punishment because she couldn't concentrate. Westchester Academy became her prison and each day all she wanted was to be liberated from it. Her mom would have been thrilled with her new attitude. If she'd known.

Now skating became her escape. It was the only time she felt free. She was reckless on the ice, skating too fast, throwing herself into her jumps and spins. And every once in a while, all that energy actually worked for her. She was skating crudely, but she was also making her double jumps more often. Occasionally she made a wild attempt at a triple. That pleased Katherine. But Ron was not happy.

"Katie, not so fast, you're all over the rink . . . ," he called out during a morning session in which she'd been even more careless than usual.

His voice irritated her. He was always correcting her, always reining her in, just when she was starting to feel good. She ignored him and picked up even more speed. She was ahead of her music now, but she didn't care. She turned to her back edge, skidding slightly because she was going at such a clip, and began the series of steps that were to launch her into her double Salchow.

"Katie, slow down," Ron called out.

"Ron, drop dead," sang the voice inside her head.

"Watch out for the barricade," Ron yelled.

She stopped herself just in time to avoid slamming into it. She grabbed it for support to keep herself from falling.

"What the hell are you trying to do?" Ron demanded as he skated over. His lips were white around the edges with anger. From up in the bleachers Katie could see her mom racing down to do some screaming.

Katherine was taking the steep steps two at a time, teetering on her thin high heels while her heavy coat flapped around her awkwardly. If she fell, Katie thought idly, she'd break her neck. Then, feeling guilty, she quickly pushed the idea out of her head.

RON AND HER mom took turns going at her. Katie heard what they said as if it were meant for someone else. A part of her knew she should be sorry—a part of her was—but it was too hard to concentrate on their words. She was fascinated by the way her mom's mouth moved. She counted the number of times Ron blinked. Mostly she just waited until they stopped making sounds. She wanted to get back to her skating. She wanted to keep moving. She could barely control her impatience with them for talking so much.

II

The feeling of impatience stayed with her through the rest of her practice session—which seemed to go on forever. Then she and her mom drove back to Westchester. She'd never noticed before what a slow driver her mother was.

When she got to school, she decided to go to her place at the end of the hall, where she could watch Dave and his buddies leave the gym. But first she had to pick up some books in her locker. That meant she wouldn't have a lot of time before her class with Ms. Moran, but she was sure she could make it if she hurried.

But the hall was full of kids—too many of them—all moving so slowly. They were getting in her way. There was no way to get around them or push through them. By the time she finally reached her locker, she wanted to scream at all of them. She yanked open the door, pulled out her books, and slammed it shut. But it bounced open again. She slammed it again. It opened again. And that was when she felt the familiar warning signals. At first, she almost didn't notice them because she was so focused on closing the door—but when her heart started beating too hard and she couldn't catch her breath, she knew what was happening. For a moment she was almost relieved, she'd been waiting for it for so long. But then she realized with terror that this time something was different. Because it was going too fast—like a reel of film playing at high speed. And there was no way to stop it. Her mind was already starting to fragment. She could feel it happening; as her mind left she was losing control faster and faster. Finally there was no way to think. Her mind was gone. All she could do was watch, as if from a long distance away, as her hand continued to slam the locker door over and over. But then she saw her other hand move between the door and the door frame. Now the door was slamming on the hand. A kid standing at the locker next to hers yelled something but Katie couldn't figure out the words. There were cuts in the skin of her hand, the blood was welling up in them. But the door went on slamming. A part of her brain warned that if this continued, she could break the bones in her hand, but she was powerless to stop it.

The kid who had yelled started backing away from her; she was vaguely aware that other kids had formed a circle around her and were watching. Somewhere in the crowd she saw Dave Malloy's face, but she was past caring. Behind her someone came through the crowd and pulled her away from the locker. Someone else tried to grab her arms, but she was too strong for them and she broke the hold. Her arms began swinging wildly; the left one was trying to repeat the motion of slamming the door on the right, even though the door was no longer within her reach. She heard Ms. Moran's voice say, "Katie, stop. Please." But then the sound was drowned out by the screams coming from her own throat.

More hands grabbed at her; other teachers had come running. They shouted at her to stop. But, of course, that was foolish. Her body twisted and turned and somehow managed to evade them. She wanted to laugh at them. But it came out more like screams.

Finally, someone managed to hold down her arms. But her shoulders pulled free and the upper part of her torso began a rhythmic motion, banging her head against the wall. Now it was her forehead that started to bleed as it hit the cinder-block wall again and again. From somewhere off in a safe place her mind registered, although she couldn't feel it, that a trickle of blood had started down one side of her face. She wished one of the teachers would wipe it away before it got on her blouse. But they were too busy shouting at her to stop—as if she could. So the blood continued down to her collar.

— ❊ —

"TRY TO GET her away from the wall," Jenny Moran yelled to Paul Georgescu as they struggled with the kicking, screaming Katie. "Pull her back so she can't hurt herself." Paul, whose chemistry lab was across the hall, had rushed over to help Jenny as she tried to subdue the child. They'd finally managed to pin her arms behind her back, but it seemed to take forever. Whatever this fit was, it had given Katie an unreal physical strength. And now that they'd managed to keep her from hurting her hand, she'd started beating her head against the wall. Finally, they managed to drag her away from it. "Katie, honey, stop it," Jenny begged. The girl turned wild, vacant eyes to meet hers.

"You can't reach her, not now," a voice at Jenny's side said grimly as Barbara Quinn grabbed Katie's shoulders. "Just try to keep her from hurting herself and let this play itself out. She'll stop by herself eventually."

KATIE KNEW IT was ending. It had subsided almost as quickly as it had begun. Suddenly her body stopped fighting and seemed to go limp. The blur around her started to become individual faces. She could see the crowd that had gathered around her. No one was saying a word. The kids and even some of the teachers were staring at her in horror. Somewhere someone snickered and the sound carried clearly in the silent hallway. Katie looked down at her bruised and bleeding hand. And she started to cry.

"Okay, people, everyone go back to your classrooms," said Mr. Georgescu.

Barbara moved in to Katie. "I'll take her down to my room," she said. "Jenny, would you come with us? I think she'll be more comfortable if you're there."

Jenny nodded. "Paul, ask the office to find someone to cover my class, will you?" she asked. She and Barbara led the sobbing Katie down the hall.

12

"We've called the mother," said Dr. Harding Kendall, the school's headmaster. He'd joined them in the nurse's station. As he spoke he shot a wary glance over at Katie, who was curled up on the cot that was in the small anteroom behind the nurse's office. The terrible racking sobbing had stopped; Katie was still crying now, but only periodically and lightly. Jennie sat in a chair next to the cot while Barbara dealt with the headmaster, who clearly would have preferred to be anywhere else. Harding had been a student at Westchester Academy back in the good old days before the sexual revolution had forced the school to admit girls as students. At this moment Jenny figured he was probably wishing he could bring back that golden past.

He indicated that Barbara should close the door to the anteroom and move their discussion to her desk. Without being asked, Jenny stood up and joined them. She'd failed Katie once when she'd listened to Ilene and backed off from helping the kid. It was not going to happen again. Neither Harding nor Barbara seemed to mind that she was there.

"Ms. Roskova is on her way," said Harding. "Pete LuRay will deal with her." Pete was the school's guidance counselor. Offhand, Jenny couldn't imagine a worse choice to handle this situation. Pete's one gift was for getting Westchester Academy students into college. Compassion wasn't his thing.

But Harding Kendall hated emotionally sticky scenes and he wasn't going to deal with this one if he could get out of it.

So the whole mess would be shuffled off to Pete LuRay and Barbara. And me, Jenny thought. She was determined to be there for Katie this time. She got the feeling that Barbara was too.

"I'm glad Ms. Roskova has been contacted," Barbara said. "Because she can give permission for the emergency medical people to take Katie to the hospital." There was a silence after this announcement. Jennie, Barbara, and Dr. Kendall all knew that the school could not sign Katie into a hospital. By law, only Katie's parents could give permission for that. "I called 911 and asked for an ambulance," Barbara explained.

Harding sighed. "Was that absolutely necessary?" he asked.

"Katie's hand should be x-rayed immediately," Barbara said firmly. "That cut on her forehead is nasty, and we can't rule out the possibility of concussion." She paused for a beat, then added, "And, of course, she should be seen by a psychiatrist."

Harding sighed again. "Yes," he said unhappily. "Although I do wish there were some other, less public way to handle this . . . It's bad enough that we've had this incident here today. I'm sure the parents of the other students will not be pleased to hear that we had police cars and ambulances outside our front door." He didn't have to add that displeased parents could mean students pulled from the school, and a loss of revenue. Barbara and Jenny exchanged a glance. Harding was always deeply concerned about the possible loss of revenue.

"It seems to me that since Katie had her attack on our premises we're liable legally as well as ethically to make every effort to get her the care she needs," Jenny offered.

"Yes, yes, yes," said Harding impatiently. "Let's just hope the mother gets here before that ambulance so we can get on with this as quickly as possible."

13

Katherine drove to the school as fast as she could with hands that were shaking as they clutched the steering wheel. She'd been on an emotional roller coaster ever since she'd been summoned to the phone by one of her colleagues at the bank. First there had been the shock of hearing from a lock-jawed male voice that Katie had been hurt in an accident at school. When she'd demanded details, the voice, which identified itself as belonging to the school's "headmaster," had become politely vague and had suggested that this was a conversation that should wait until she arrived at the academy. Dr. Kendall then reassured her that Katie's injuries were not serious and managed to get himself off the phone before she could question him further.

In a panic, Katherine had told her supervisor what had happened, left the bank, and begun driving as fast as she could to the academy. At first, her imagination ran wild. From what Dr. Kendall had said it seemed safe to assume Katie's injuries were not life-threatening. But that still left plenty of room for disaster. A cold fish like the "headmaster" spoke a different language than she did—so God knew what he meant when he said an injury wasn't serious. And even if Katie wasn't badly hurt, something as minor as a sprained ankle could mean the end of everything for a skater facing the junior championships. Katherine gripped the steering wheel so tightly her knuckles hurt—surely God wouldn't let that happen. Not after they'd worked so hard and come so close.

— ❋ —

SHE WAS GETTING near the school now. It was only about
five blocks away. As she turned the corner onto the street
where it was, she could feel her mouth start to get dry and
she began to sweat the way she had when she was a kid and
her mother took her to one of the big houses she cleaned.
Although Katherine would never have admitted it to anyone,
Westchester Academy always had that effect on her. Just the
sight of it brought back her own horrible years in high
school.

She'd grown up in an outlying area of New Haven, Connecticut. The social life at her school had been dominated by
kids Katherine privately named "The Americans"—blonde
kids whose mothers didn't speak with an accent or have to
work. The girls wore matching sweater sets and penny
loafers. The guys drove their own cars. And they all looked
down on kids like Katherine Petolovski. Except during the
winter when everyone went skating at Gregson's outdoor
rink. That was when Katherine shone. She worked at Gregson's as a guard, skating around the large outdoor pond to
help little kids who had fallen or to warn off hotshots who
were going too close to the thin ice. But whenever it wasn't
busy at the rink, the figure-skating pro gave her pointers. He
said she was a natural at the sport, with a talent that was
God-given.

Katherine lived for the winters. And for the annual visits
of the Ice Follies and the Ice Capades to the New Haven
Arena. Sometimes she managed to scrape up enough money
to see the shows every night they were in town. She sat in
the bleachers and watched as glittering gods and goddesses
swooped and swirled under spotlights, making real life van-
ish for a few glorious hours. She studied their mannerisms
and styles, incorporating whatever she could into her own
skating at the rink. Then, when the kids from school showed
up at Gregson's, she always found a way to show off her new
tricks. She knew she was a better skater than the girls who
had fancy lessons at the skating club in town. Sometimes
they would ask her for help on a spin or spiral—she always

gave it graciously. Once, she'd taught the dentist's daughter, Mindy Fairchild, to do a mohawk turn, and Mrs. Fairchild, who was one of her mother's employers, had mentioned it when her mother came to clean. That night her mother had slapped her hard across the face to remind her not to get above herself.

THE SCHOOL LOOMED up ahead, its big stone entrance as formidable as ever. Katherine was always amazed at the ease with which Katie went in and out of this place. Of course, Katie could do it because she had the ice-skating. That was what made her as good as anyone else here. And since Katherine was the ice-skater's mother, she could walk in with her head high too.

She drove into the parking lot and was about to get out of her car when she saw the flashing red lights. Then she realized that they were on top of a police car, and no—please, God, no—an ambulance. She got out of the car and began to run.

14

"Ms. Roskova, I'm afraid I have to insist," said Mr. LuRay. Katie smiled weakly to herself as she listened to him. So far, the debate between the guidance counselor and her mom was a draw. Katie was still lying on the cot, but the door to the nurse's office was open now so she could follow what was going on. Listening was kind of fun, she decided dreamily. It was like watching a championship competition; the winner would be the one who racked up the most points after the judges had given out the scores.

When her mom had first come bursting into the nurse's office, Katie could tell how scared she was. But then, after she'd had a good look at Katie's minor injuries, she'd started to get mad. Katie knew she was thinking about the time she was losing from work and the possibility that they might have to miss the afternoon practice session. Also, this whole scene was embarrassing her, and her mom really hated that. So naturally, she started being nasty to everyone. And when Mr. LuRay asked her to sign the permission form so that the ambulance could take Katie to the emergency room at the hospital, she refused. I could have told them she would, Katie thought.

She felt so lazy, she couldn't seem to make herself care who won the competition. Somewhere vaguely in the back of her mind she knew the outcome would be important for her. But her head was aching so much it was hard to think. The best she could do was listen. It seemed to be her mom's turn to talk again.

"Katie has a few little scratches and a bump on her head," she said. "She'll be fine by tomorrow—"

"Ms. Roskova," said Mr. LuRay, "as I've tried to tell you repeatedly, our concern is not just with Katie's physical injuries, but her behavior. When a child has an episode like the one she just had, we know she's in trouble. . . ."

Katie frowned. Her recollection of what had happened in the hallway was a little dim. It felt as if it had all happened a long time ago.

"Katie had an accident—"

"Her injuries were self-inflicted and in no way accidental. Your daughter had some sort of an attack in our school, Ms. Roskova." Mr. LuRay droned on. It was too bad that he was short and had a whiny voice, Katie thought. Her mother would have responded better to Dr. Kendall's height and deep baritone.

"We must know more about what caused your daughter's outburst," Mr. LuRay was saying. "I know I don't have to remind you that Katie is here on scholarship and we have the right to ask questions about her ability to continue functioning as a student."

The threat of a pulled scholarship worth fifteen thousand dollars a year got to her mom. Katie could tell because Katherine's face got very red. Good move, Mr. LuRay, Katie congratulated him silently. I'd give you a score of 9.9 on that one.

"Are you threatening me, Mr. LuRay?" Katherine asked. "Are you saying you won't give Katie her scholarship if I don't sign this form?" It was exactly what he was doing, of course, but it sounded so much nicer the way he said it. Katie could see him backing off a little. Too bad, she thought. For a while he'd had a shot at the gold, but now he was blowing it.

Then, without warning, Ms. Moran stepped in to say, "The scholarship is not the point, Ms. Roskova," and Katie felt herself stiffen. It was one thing for Katie to joke to herself about her mom losing the competition to Mr. LuRay, but this was serious. A woman like Ms. Moran—young, pretty, and well-educated—would bring out the worst in Katherine. Katie watched her mother's mouth set in a stubborn line as Ms. Moran went on. "You can't ignore what happened here today," she said angrily. "Katie should be seen and evaluated by a professional. She needs help."

Katie knew her mom had stopped hearing the words that were being said. All Katherine felt now was the criticism leveled at her by the young woman in front of her.

"I know what my daughter needs," Katherine said loudly. "I don't need you to tell me what to do . . ." Katie tried to pull herself up to a sitting position. Her mom was capable of losing it and doing something stupid, and Katie couldn't let her expose herself that way. Not in front of these people. Because afterward her mom would feel so humiliated. Somehow Katie had to protect her from that. She was trying to figure out what to do when Ms. Moran said, "As far as I'm concerned, if you don't let Katie go to the emergency room for a complete checkup, it'll be a case of neglect and I'll have to report it to the authorities."

"That will not be necessary, Ms. Moran," said a voice behind them, and Dr. Kendall walked in. "Westchester Academy will report the incident if we do not feel that Katie is getting the attention she needs." He gave Katherine a chilly smile that had to make her feel like dirt. Katie cringed. "I'm sure Ms. Roskova can understand our position. The laws of New York State that address child abuse are very clear. We'd be liable ourselves for charges if we didn't report a clear case of neglect."

For a minute Katie thought her mother was going to let Dr. Kendall have it. She was pulling herself up to her full height and breathing deeply the way she usually did before she attacked someone. But then the headmaster's quiet air of authority got to her. She sagged like a balloon that had had all the air let out of it. "Oh, all right," she said. Her face was still tight and pinched, which meant she was angry, but she signed the form.

15

"Miss, we've been here for forty-five minutes," Katherine complained to the clerk at the admitting desk. It was her third return trip to it since they'd checked in, and the woman looked annoyed.

"Lady, I've already told you you're a third-level priority. You're not a life-threatening injury or chest pains. Now please take your seat and we'll call you when we're ready."

"I don't have time for this," Katherine said, but she did as she was told. "Some people have to work for a living," she added as a parting shot. She sat down next to Katie. She hadn't spoken to her daughter since they'd arrived at the hospital, which was unusual, given how angry Katie knew she had to be. She wondered if her mother was a little scared. But then Katherine turned to her. "Throwing a tantrum like that wasn't very smart," she said. "Those people at your school don't understand artistic temperament."

So that was how they were going to explain what had happened, Katie thought. Well, maybe her mom was right. She had been feeling high-strung lately. So maybe her temper had just flared up a little—and it really wasn't anything more serious than that. For a moment she thought about trying to tell her mother about the rest of it—the spacing out and lack of control. But she decided against it. Katherine wouldn't want to know.

So mother and daughter sat together in silence. And Katie felt herself getting more and more nervous. She was still tired; her hand throbbed and her head ached; but none of that mattered. Because she was waiting for something to happen. The problem was, she didn't know what. She looked around her. On television, the emergency rooms were always full of shouting doctors and nurses and mangled patients on gurneys. When she'd arrived at the hospital, she'd been afraid she'd have to see that stuff. But nothing much seemed to be happening here at all. Earlier there had been some excitement when an old lady who was having trouble breathing was brought in by her family. A woman who seemed to be her daughter cried and looked very scared while two orderlies raced out, put the sick woman in a wheelchair, and whisked her off behind closed double doors at the far end of the room. Then the daughter sat in a metal chair near the double doors and sobbed while a man patted her awkwardly on the head. Finally a nurse came out and told the couple to follow her, and they went behind the doors themselves and that was the last Katie saw of them.

But even though the emergency room wasn't anything like what Katie had expected, it still scared her. It was a serious place for people who were really sick. She didn't want to be there any more than her mom did.

"Thanks to your little fit, your fancy-dancy school principal treated me like I was the worst mother in the world. I didn't appreciate that," complained the sharp voice at her side.

"He's called a headmaster," Katie said. She knew it would drive her mother up a wall to be corrected like that, but suddenly that was what she wanted to do. "Go ahead, Mom," commanded the voice inside her head. "Flip out and start tossing things around the emergency room. Let them see who's really crazy in the family."

But then she stole a look at Katherine, sitting next to her. Her makeup had caked in the lines on the sides of her mouth, making the crevices seem even deeper than they were. In the harsh fluorescent light, her mother looked old. "I'm sorry, Mama," Katie said softly as she touched her sleeve. She hadn't called Katherine Mama since she was a little kid.

"Katie Roskova," a nurse with a clipboard called out. She pulled herself to her feet as Katherine stood up next to her. They followed the woman through the double doors.

They were led to a big room with a row of hospital beds along one wall. Each of the beds had curtains around it like walls, but none of them had been pulled shut. Obviously, privacy wasn't a top priority in this place. There was more activity in this area than in the waiting room. They passed a man in a wheelchair who was heavily bandaged and moaning to himself. People wearing open-backed hospital gowns sat on beds or chairs answering doctors' and nurses' questions, while friends and relatives stood back, looking worried. One lady who was so white she was kind of green had a tube in her nose. A paging system called out names constantly, but no one seemed to pay any attention. Opposite the beds there was a cluster of desks, all of which overflowed with charts and folders.

The nurse stopped at one of the beds and said, "Take off your sweater and your blouse, and hop up on this. A doctor will see you in a few minutes."

Katie stiffened. And she realized why she'd been so afraid of this place—the examination. She'd been so tired, and so much had happened, she'd completely forgotten that a doctor would actually have to look at her arm.

Of course she had to have a physical exam every year for school, but for that she went to old Dr. Winnesaug, who had been her pediatrician. All he ever did was take her pulse, and check her ears and throat, the way he'd been doing since she was in kindergarten. He'd never ask her to take off her blouse. And even if she were to hold her bare arm up in front of him so the scars were in plain sight, he'd probably refuse to recognize what they were. And he'd never, ever believe that sweet little Katie Roskova had given them to herself.

But here in the hospital it would be different. There would be a doctor who hadn't known her since she was born. The doctor here would really look at her. She wasn't worried about the cut on her breast; it was hidden beneath her bra. But when she took off her blouse, the marks on her arm would be visible. The doctor would know what she'd been doing. And then it would all be over. The people at the hospital would find a way to make her tell her secrets. The walls around the compartments that were so necessary to her survival would fall.

She knew she'd jeopardized the secrets when she banged her hand with the locker door, but she was sure she could cover herself on that. "It happened one time because I got upset," she'd say with a smile. "It'll never happen again." The adults would accept it because grown-ups always believed what was easiest when it came to kids. But letting them see the scars was different. The scars protected the secrets. Everything depended on keeping them safe.

She forced herself to do her best smile. "Do I have to get undressed?" she asked in a voice that she meant to sound casual but that came out scared and whispery.

"Just your blouse and jacket, so the doctor can get a good look at you," said the nurse kindly. She was definitely the motherly type.

"But it's so cold in here, and if they just want to see my hand—" she began.

"Katie, don't give her a hard time, just do it," said her mother.

The nurse gave her mom a look that said Katherine was being insensitive, then turned back to Katie. "Why don't I close the curtains for you, honey?" she asked gently. "And I'll bring you a hospital gown. Will that make you more comfortable?" Obviously, she thought the problem was that Katie was too modest to undress in public. Katie thought fast.

"Would it be okay . . ." she began hesitantly, then she looked down at the floor as if she were too shy to look the nurse in the eye. "Would it be all right—I mean, could I put my blouse over the gown?" She made her voice an embarrassed whisper. "Those gowns are open in the back," she added as if it was all too painful.

"Katie, for God's sake . . ." her mother protested.

It was the most helpful thing her mother could have done.

"I don't see any problem with letting you throw your

blouse over your hospital gown, honey," said the nurse. She gave Katherine another dirty look.

Katie breathed a sigh of relief. She would indeed "throw on" her long-sleeved blouse over her hospital robe. And she would leave the front unfastened so it would look casual. But she was going to button the wrists. The blouse would cover the scars.

16

A woman doctor conducted the examination. She was tall and skinny and very cheerful.

"Hi there. I'm Dr. Baydee," she said. According to the plastic name tag on her white coat, her first name was Allison. "Okay, now, let's see what we've got here," she said as she began checking out the cut over Katie's eyebrow and her swollen forehead. "Thank goodness you have a hard head, right?" She laughed as if she had just cracked a joke. Katie forced a little snicker. "The good news is, you banged the front of your head and not the back," Dr. Baydee chirped as she made rapid notes on a clipboard. "The forehead is the toughest part of the skull. We'll have to stitch up that cut over your eye, but I can almost guarantee that you don't have a concussion." It seemed to make her very happy. She beamed at Katie and Katherine. Then she began examining Katie's hand.

"No broken bones," she announced gaily. "Although I am going to send you down to X ray just to be on the safe side. And I will have to close up that cut." There was an ugly-looking wound on the back of Katie's hand where the jagged edge of the locker door had torn into the skin. "But all in all, I'd say we got off lightly," the doctor added.

What do you mean "we"? Katie thought. She resented the way the perky doctor was talking down to her. Adults didn't usually treat Katie Roskova as if she were a three-year-old. On the plus side, it seemed more than likely that this woman was another one of the upbeat types who didn't want to believe a pretty, bright young girl could have terrible secrets. So perhaps if she was handled right, she wouldn't look any farther than the injuries she could see. Katie smiled at her. "Oh, yes," she agreed heartily. "We got off real lightly."

"I'll just get a nurse in here and we'll start patching you up." She didn't ask to see Katie's arms. The scars were safe. So far.

It took four stitches to fix the cut on her forehead. When the doctor took out the nasty-looking curved needle she was going to use, Katie saw Katherine pale under her makeup and turn away. She stared intently at the opposite corner of the cubicle, trying to look calm, but Katie could see that she was swallowing hard.

"Would you like me to give you a shot of Novocain?" the doctor asked Katie.

"No thanks," said Katie. "I'll be fine." Out of the corner of her eye she saw Katherine shudder slightly. Katie couldn't resist flashing a quick smile at the back of her mother's head. "Who's the tough one now, Mom?" asked the voice inside her mind.

The stitches felt like pinpricks. "You're a brave girl," said the nurse.

"Just do it and let me get out of here," Katie commanded her silently. She wanted to get away before the doctor got any clever ideas about examining her. She pressed her arm against her side. Even though her blouse covered the scars, she wasn't taking any chances.

Fixing her hand was easier for the doctor than taking care of the cut on her forehead.

"I think we can get away without stitches here," the doctor announced. "This cut isn't as deep as the one on your forehead." Katie looked down at the wound. It zigzagged across the back of her hand, which was now so swollen it looked deformed. Katie saw Katherine sneak a sidelong glance, then quickly turn away again.

"Please put your hand on the table, and turn it over so I can check the fingers," said the doctor. "And would you please unbutton your sleeve?" Katie felt herself start to panic. The table was about a foot and a half away. There was no way to do what Dr. Baydee was asking without stretching out her arm. If her sleeve was unbuttoned, it could slide up as she stretched, and the doctor would see the scars—or at least she could see them if she happened to be looking. The possibility was too close for comfort. She had to keep the scars covered . . .

But if she refused to do as she'd been asked, the doctor and her mother would know something was wrong. So how was she going to handle this? She looked over at Katherine, who was still turned away, unable to watch. So far so good. As for Dr. Baydee, Katie had already written her off as kind of dumb. Cautiously, Katie put her hand out as far as she could while still keeping the arm pressed safely against her body. It was an awkward position, but if she bent forward and hunched over, she could just reach the table. She waited for the doctor to ask why she had twisted herself into the shape of a pretzel. But the woman didn't seem to care. She examined Katie's hand for a few seconds, then relinquished it.

"I was right," she said finally with her bright smile. "No stitches needed. We'll just close the cut with a few butterfly tapes."

Katie pulled her hand back and straightened up. She waited for the trap to spring. She couldn't believe the doctor hadn't noticed how weirdly she was acting. But the doctor seemed blissfully unaware that anything was wrong. She even hummed a little as she cleaned the wound and taped it together with little pieces of surgical tape that looked like two triangles connected at the points. The swelling had caused the wound to open farther, so the doctor had to hold it closed before she taped.

"Am I hurting you?" she murmured without even looking up to see Katie shake her head. Finally, she wrapped up her handiwork with layers of white gauze.

"Don't get it wet, and make sure it stays wrapped until I see you again," said the doctor. "Plan to come back in a week."

Katie nodded and quickly rebuttoned her sleeve. She was

barely able to contain her relief. It was over. She'd kept the scars hidden; the secrets and the walls were still in place. She got off the bed. Katherine was at her side in a flash. For once Katie and her mother were on the same wavelength.

"Let's go," said Katherine.

"Oh, we're not through yet," said the doctor. "Katie, suppose you tell me how this happened." She was still smiling as she leaned back, as if she had all the time in the world. Katie felt a surge of anger. The ordeal was over, and she'd won. Why was the doctor dragging it out?

"I lost my temper," she said, stealing the idea from her mother.

The doctor nodded and wrote something down on the chart. She mumbled her next words so softly Katie almost missed them. But she didn't.

"Now before you go," said the doctor, "I'd like to take a look at your arm. Could you take off your blouse, please?"

Katie stared at the woman blankly. For a second she wondered if her imagination was playing tricks on her.

"You're holding your arm as if it hurts," said the doctor with an encouraging smile. "I just want to see what's going on."

"It doesn't hurt," said Katie desperately. "It's okay . . ."

But the doctor reached out her hand for the blouse. "I'll hang it up for you," she said cheerfully.

There was nothing to do but take off her blouse.

"Go away, go away, go away," screamed the voice in her head.

The doctor grasped her arm. Katie glanced over at her mother, who was looking off into space again. She really doesn't want to deal with any of this, Katie thought. What Mom doesn't want to know, Mom doesn't know. She tried to press her arm to her side. But the doctor was holding it.

"Relax," she said with a smile. Then she turned the arm over. The scars were right under her nose. There was no way she could miss them. Katie held her breath and waited for the inevitable questions—and recriminations.

But nothing happened. The doctor glanced so quickly at her arm, Katie wasn't sure she'd even seen the scars. Was it possible that she hadn't? Katie wanted to scream the question at her. Instead, she waited silently for the doctor to say something.

But she didn't. She didn't look surprised, she didn't frown. She didn't even write anything on her clipboard.

"Okay, that's it," she said. She was still smiling.

Katie forced herself not to grab her blouse. She picked it up casually and put it on slowly.

Katherine turned around with a sigh of relief. "Can we get out of here now?" she demanded. Of course, she hadn't seen the scars.

"First, Katie has to go to X ray," the doctor said. She added to Katie, "The nurse will take you."

Katie nodded. I got away with it, she thought. Somehow, miraculously, the doctor hadn't seen the scars. Katie couldn't believe it. Nothing was going to happen. For some reason, that made her want to cry.

"When you come back from X ray," the doctor continued, "we'll want you to have a talk with our psychiatric resident, Dr. Karachi."

Once again Katie wasn't sure if she'd imagined what she'd heard. The doctor said it as if it were no big deal. But Katie knew what the word "psychiatric" meant—they were sending her to a shrink. Shrinks were trained to poke around in people's minds and figure out their thoughts. You couldn't lie to a shrink. You couldn't keep secrets from them.

At her side, Katherine gasped angrily. "What?" she demanded. "Katie doesn't need to see a psychiatrist."

"Oh yes she does," said the doctor firmly, without a trace of her sunny smile. "It's hospital policy. And in a case like this, it's also the law. Your daughter came in here because she injured herself while in an emotionally disturbed state. Under those circumstances, we automatically do a psychiatric evaluation. In fact, we won't release her without one."

Katie wanted to cry. As the nurse led her off to X ray, she thought, I've lost.

17

They wouldn't let her mother be present for the "talk" with Dr. Karachi. Katherine fought with them about it, but there wasn't anything she could do.

"It's a hospital rule," said the nurse who brought Katie back from the x-ray room. "Psychiatric interviews with minors are always done without parents present."

So Katherine was forced to go back to the waiting room while Katie returned to sit on the bed in the same cubicle where the smiley doctor had treated her wounds.

The bed was so high that her feet dangled as she looked around at the curtained "walls." She was on her own for the first time in her life. Before this, whenever she'd had to face anything big, Katherine had been with her. She was usually yelling at Katie—but she was there.

Now Katie was going to have to deal with this shrink alone. Mind over matter, she told herself, and forced herself to sit straight and tall. This won't be so bad, she told herself. After the X ray they'd let her put her blouse back on. So at least the scars were safe.

The first thing Katie noticed when Dr. Karachi finally walked in was that he looked tired. He didn't seem to be too old, but it was hard to tell because there were such dark circles under his eyes. He was small and skinny, with black hair and eyes; his complexion was a light, creamy brown. Katie figured he came from someplace like India or Pakistan. He didn't say anything to her but went straight to the foot of the bed as if she weren't there. He picked up a clipboard and began studying it. Finally he moved to her and spoke in a soft, heavily accented voice.

"I am Dr. Karachi," he said and held out his hand. Katie shook it formally and held back a nervous giggle. He didn't seem to notice and went back to reading his chart.

"What are you going to do to me?" screamed the voice inside her head. "Get on with it."

As if he'd heard her, he suddenly looked up. "Now, then," he said, "can you tell me the day of the week?"

She looked at him, not sure what he was talking about.

"Do you know what today is?" he prompted.

"It's Monday," she ventured. The answer seemed to satisfy him.

"Do you know the date and the year?"

She couldn't believe it; after everything she'd been through, this little guy was playing a guessing game with her . . . "What are you doing, you fool?" screamed the voice in her head. But she told him the date and the year. After which he asked her the name of the President and made her count backward from a hundred by sevens. When she got to seventy-two, he stopped her and wrote something on her chart.

"What is this?" the voice in her head shouted at him. "What's going on?"

He finished writing and looked up at her with eyes that had no expression in them. "Now perhaps you will tell me how the injuries to your hand occurred," he said in a flat tone.

"I was trying to close my locker and my hand got hit with the door." She'd meant to say it better than that and to smile at him to let him see it was all kind of funny. But he was making her so nervous, she forgot.

"It says on your chart your injuries were self-inflicted," he noted.

"I got upset because I couldn't get the door closed. I was late for class and my locker was full of junk . . ." She tried the smile, but he was too busy looking at his chart again to see it.

"Do you have problems at home?" he asked. She was about to answer, but to her amazement, he turned away and stifled a yawn. She stared at him. She was killing herself trying to answer him and he was yawning.

"Sorry," he said with an apologetic smile. "I have been working on a double shift. No sleep for twenty-four hours. Now tell me about your home. Are there problems?"

"No," she said sullenly. He didn't pick up on her change in attitude.

"Do you have a boyfriend?"

"Nope."

"At school, have you failed any examinations lately?"

"I never get less than an A minus, you jerk," said the voice in her head. "No," she said out loud.

"So there is no reason why you should have become so upset that you hurt yourself?"

"No."

"Do you hurt yourself often?"

She hesitated, then said, "No, I don't."

He looked at her sharply for the first time. "In your chart it says you have many scars."

That was when she realized how they had worked together to catch her. The smiley doctor had reported the scars after all. And then this one had deliberately lulled her into a false sense of security with his crazy mind games. She should have known she couldn't trust any of the people in this place.

"May I see your arm, please?" he asked.

"I don't—" she began, but Dr. Karachi took her arm firmly, turned it so the under part was exposed to the light, and pulled up her sleeve. There they were again—the white-and-red lines in her skin. Her scars. Her secret.

Dr. Karachi stared at her arm for what seemed like a very long time. She had no doubt that he saw what was there—and that he knew exactly what it meant.

Instinctively she tried to pull her arm back, but he was holding it too tightly. She wanted to scream that he had no right to do this—her scars were private, they were not meant for his eyes—but she felt so humiliated she couldn't open her mouth. She yanked her arm again, and this time he let it go. She pulled it in to hold it against her side. But it was too late to regain her dignity. This was worse than being naked. She felt tears start to well up in her eyes and she tried to blink them back. She wanted to disappear. She wanted to die. Dr. Karachi looked at her impassively. It was impossible to tell what he was thinking.

"You have been doing this for a while," he finally said in his flat tone. "You are hurting yourself on purpose out of some emotional need. If you do not wish to get psychiatrically sicker, it will be necessary for you to see a therapist on a regular basis."

She wanted to ask him what the words "psychiatrically sicker" meant. She wanted him to say that he wasn't disgusted by what he'd found out about her. He was the first person aside from the woman doctor who had ever seen her scars. He was the only person who had ever spoken to her about them. She needed him to say something a little bit kind.

Instead, he stood up. "Well, you can go home now," he said. She tried to look up at him. "Please tell me I'm going to be okay," the voice in her head begged him. "Please talk to me." But her eyes were too full of tears, so she turned away. She didn't want him to see.

"I hope you will consider what I've just told you," he said. "If you do not get help, you will be back here. Probably, you will keep coming back for the rest of your life." For a moment she thought she saw something like concern in his dark eyes, and she thought he was going to say something to make her feel better. But he looked back at his clipboard instead. "I will make a strong recommendation that you receive treatment in my report," he said. "Good luck to you." And he walked out.

She wouldn't let herself sob out loud because there was no point. Certainly, the doctor wouldn't care. She was sick, he'd said. She would get worse, and she would come back to this place again. That was going to be her life.

Finally, she started getting dressed. Before she left the cubicle she pulled down her sleeve very carefully over her scars.

18

"We got off easier than I thought we would," said Katherine when they got home. "We've lost the afternoon's practice and Ron will charge me for your lesson, but things could have been a lot worse. So we're going to forget this ever happened. Do you hear me? It never happened."

Katie nodded, but the scary words "psychiatrically sick" were still echoing in her head. "The doctor said I had to go to therapy—" she began weakly.

"He *recommended* it. It's in that damn report I'm gonna have to send to your school," said Katherine. Then she paused, something obviously bothering her. "The doctor also tried to tell me something about some scars . . . on your arms . . . I couldn't make out what he was saying with that accent of his . . . some nonsense about you hurting yourself."

It was a chance to level with her mother—maybe it was even her opportunity to try to get the "help" Dr. Karachi had said she needed. But one look at her mom's face told her how much Katherine would not want to hear the truth. She was waiting for Katie to come up with an explanation that would make this potentially disturbing thing go away. And Katie knew she had to do it. Her first responsibility was to her mother—no matter how much the threat of psychiatric sickness had scared her.

"I know what he was talking about," she said. "He found the scar from the stitches I had after I fell doing the double Salchow." The stitches had been far up on her arm, almost at her shoulder, and the scar they left bore no resemblance to those on her forearm, but Katherine nodded eagerly. Obviously, if Dr. Karachi had described the scars on Katie's forearm she hadn't understood him. Or she hadn't wanted to understand him. "I told him, sometimes I fall when I skate," Katie went on. "He must have gotten it into his head that I hurt myself. And then when I had the temper tantrum . . . well, I guess he thinks I'm too accident-prone or something."

"So let him pay for therapy," said Katherine. "I've got better things to do with my money." She looked at Katie with resentment. "We wouldn't be having these problems with all these busybodies if you'd kept your temper. When I was your age, if I'd flown off the handle the way you did and disgraced my parents, my father would have given me therapy all right—he'd have beaten me until I couldn't sit down for a week. So just thank your lucky stars I'm not him, and go do your homework for tomorrow."

It was the first time Katie had thought about facing the kids at school. "Couldn't I stay home for a couple of days?" she begged.

Katherine knew what was going through her mind. "So you can give everyone a chance to forget the spectacle you made of yourself? Absolutely not. I know it'll be hard for you when you go back, but you should have thought of that before you decided to lose your temper."

Katie knew there was no way she could concentrate enough to study, but she dutifully opened her books. She was trying with no success to focus on her math assignment when the phone rang and Katherine picked it up. Seconds later she heard her mother say, "But, Dr. Kendall, Katie's fine," and she gave up all pretense of working and listened. The conversation was fast; her mother's side of it seemed limited to saying, "I don't think that's any of your business," and, "I have the report, I'll bring it to the school," before she slammed down the receiver.

She stood in front of Katie. "I hope you're happy," she said in a voice that was hoarse with fury. "That was your principal—I mean your 'headmaster.' They don't want you back in school until they see your hospital report. Then they're going to 'assess your continued relationship with the academy.' "

Katie couldn't believe they were thinking about dumping her. "But I never get less than an A minus," she whispered.

"Do you think anyone cares about that when you do crazy things like banging your head against a wall?" her mother yelled. "Why did you do it? You know we've got to have that damn school for the skating. Why do you want to ruin everything we've been working for? Answer me."

"I don't know," said Katie dully.

"Psychiatrically sick," said the voice in her head.

19

"I've talked to the mother and it's clear that she has no intention of seeking any kind of therapeutic help for Katie," said Harding Kendall.

Katie's emotional breakdown in the hallway had occurred three days ago, and the school—meaning Kendall—had not yet decided whether to allow her to come back. Finally, the headmaster had gathered a small group into his office to thrash the matter out with him. He'd asked Pete LuRay, Ilene Santiago, and Barbara Quinn, who had asked Jenny to come along. "I have a feeling you and I are going to have to stand up for Katie," she said.

So far, Kendall had done most of the talking.

"The question is, should Katie continue here at Westchester Academy?" he said. "We don't want to be unfair to her but we do have a responsibility to the other students and their parents. According to the hospital report, Katie has serious emotional problems, which have been going on for some time."

"So we just kick her out because she's not a perfect specimen?" demanded Jenny.

"You don't understand what's involved here," said Ilene. She'd come to the meeting prepared, with notes on a pad. She referred to them briefly.

"Katie is a sick little girl," she said. "Technically speaking, there's no real name for her illness. It's a form of psychosis. In the vernacular, she's what we call a self-mutilator. That means pretty much what it sounds like—a kid who injures herself. It can take many forms; these kids burn themselves, they bang their hands and fingers until they break them, but most commonly they cut their own skin. According to the hospital report, Katie has scars up and down both forearms, which indicate that this is what she does."

"She told me she fell a lot and scraped her arms during her skating practices," said Jenny. Less than a month ago she'd been arguing with Ilene that this couldn't be true. But now that such a grim label had been put on Katie, she wanted to believe the girl's story about injuries that had occurred as a result of overtraining.

"We're not talking about accidents," said Ilene. "You suspected that Katie was lying to you about that, and you were right. This kid deliberately inflicts harm on her own body because she gets a kind of catharsis from the pain." She paused briefly, then added, "Katie may also be into the sight of her own blood. These kids are comforted by pain. The blood comes to symbolize that comfort for them—it actually soothes them." A little grimace of distaste played at the corners of her mouth as she said the words.

Jenny felt herself shudder, but she fought it. "Look," she said, "whatever Katie does, she needs help. We can't abandon her."

" 'Abandon' is an unnecessarily melodramatic term," said Harding. "We're simply trying to make the best choice for the school."

"And I don't see where the school will be served by losing one of its best students," Jenny argued. "Katie hasn't hurt anyone but herself."

"That little display with the locker door was very disturbing," said Pete.

"Maybe it was a call for help," said Barbara. "The poor kid must be in a lot of pain to act out in this way."

"Westchester Academy is not in the business of offering that kind of help," said Pete crisply.

"Maybe we should be," Barbara shot back.

"Ilene, what are the chances of Katie going off the deep end again?" asked Harding.

Ilene shrugged her exquisite shoulders. "Who knows?" she said. "Essentially, self-mutilation is a coping mechanism for a kid who doesn't have any other way to handle her feelings. When her stress is too great, the pain gives her something to focus on. Strange as it may sound, it actually calms her down. What you saw Katie do to herself with the locker door is just an extreme version of the kind of harm she regularly inflicts on herself in private.

"Just about anything could set her off. And I wouldn't even try to predict whether her next incident will be played out in front of the entire student body or whether she'll simply go off to indulge in a little private bloodletting."

"In other words, if Katie stays with us, we could have a repeat of the experience of last week."

"Probably. Especially if she's not in therapy. I'll be honest with you, Harding, I've never treated one of these kids. But as I understand it, hurting yourself can become a stubborn little habit if it goes on for any length of time. Furthermore, the kids who do it are at risk for a whole grab bag of other problems, including substance abuse and eating disorders."

"Who needs it?" Pete muttered under his breath.

"So what we're going to do to a kid who's at risk for all kind of serious emotional problems is cut the ground out from under her," said Jenny. "How do you think Katie's going to feel if we reject her like this? Just for one lousy mistake?"

"Jenny, please," Harding broke in with elaborate patience. "If this girl were in treatment, I'd be a lot more comfortable keeping her on. But her mother refuses to hear of it. So we're faced with a youngster who has an ongoing psychological disorder and a mother who will not consider therapy for her."

"I say we let her become someone else's problem," Pete tossed in.

"What if, instead of pulling the scholarship and forcing Katie to leave, we use it as leverage with the mother," said Jenny. "We could tell Ms. Roskova the only way Katie can stay here is if she's in therapy. Say we'll take away the scholarship if she's not. That way we'll actually be able to do some good for Katie, and we can protect the school too."

"Just try it for a couple of months, Harding," urged Barbara. "If there are more problems with Katie, you can still ask her to leave, but at least we'll all know we haven't deserted the child when she is at her most vulnerable."

"We do have some responsibility to her," said Jenny. "I don't think it will hurt us with the other parents if we give her a second chance. In fact, it might make us look good. Remember, she's still a kid with a very interesting future."

Harding looked from Jenny to Ilene. "Ilene," he said finally, "could you recommend a good therapist for Katie?"

"I'm sure I could find someone," said Ilene.

"Would it be appropriate for you to speak with her first?" he asked.

For a fraction of a second, the psychologist hesitated. Jenny was sure she could pick up the same feeling of distaste she'd sensed earlier. But Ilene seemed to pull herself out of it quickly.

"Of course," she said smoothly. "That way I'd have a much better feel for Katie's needs. Although I do think it would be more comfortable for her if we didn't do it on the school grounds. I have an office here in town for my private practice."

The look of relief on Harding's face was almost funny, Jenny thought. He was thrilled to be able to dump this girl with her unpleasant problem on someone—anyone—else.

"How quickly can you see her, Ilene? I think the sooner the better, don't you?"

Ilene consulted an appointment book that she fished out of her expensive leather handbag. "How about tomorrow morning?"

"That sounds fine. I'll have my secretary call Ms. Roskova today and set it up," Harding said as he flashed a quick smile in Ilene's direction. Jenny thought the smile Ilene flashed back was a little forced. If Ilene could have found a graceful way of refusing to deal with Katie and her problem, Jenny was sure she would have. Poor Katie, thought Jenny. The kid had been sitting at home for three days waiting for a group of adults to decide her fate. Now we're going to fob her off on Ilene, who can't even think about her without shuddering. I wish we could do better by you, Katie, she thought.

20

The three days that followed the episode in the school hall-way were awful for Katie. The morning after it happened, she woke up early, before her alarm went off, with a head that ached and a hand that throbbed. The sight of her face in the bathroom mirror made her gasp. The right side of her forehead and her right eye were swollen and purple. The blood from the cut over her eyebrow had seeped through the bandage. The eye itself was so puffy it was almost closed, and there was a red scrape like a carpet burn along her cheek. Without thinking, she raised her injured hand to touch it. The hand was also swollen under the white ban-dage. While she was staring at herself, her mother appeared in the doorway behind her.

Katherine seemed to have gotten over her rage of the night before.

"Here," she said, holding out a bottle of her own thick makeup foundation. "Put this on over that shiner."

Katie began slathering the makeup over the bruises. It made them look worse—the purple appeared even darker and meaner-looking. Katherine didn't seem to notice; she was too busy mapping out the game plan for Katie's unex-pected mini-vacation.

"Since that school of yours says you can't go back for a while, we might as well make the most of it," she said briskly. "You can stay at the rink all day and work out between your lessons. Maybe Ron can give you some more time."

— ❀ —

BUT IT HADN'T worked out that way. When they'd arrived at the rink, Ron had taken one startled look at Katie's swollen face and bandaged hand, and he'd sent her home.

"A fall could reopen the cuts, and we'd be in real trouble," he'd told Katherine when she'd tried to argue with him. "I want her to take the rest of the week off to heal up."

What bothered Katie the most was the way he'd looked at her as he said it. There was a mixture of concern and something else she couldn't quite read—maybe suspicion—in his gaze.

"What the hell happened to you?" he asked her. Before Katie could answer, Katherine stepped in. "Katie tripped and fell down some stairs at school," she'd said with a fake chuckle. "Can you believe it? A championship skater who's a complete klutz."

"Well, when you take off the skates, life can get pretty dangerous," Ron had joked back. But Katie could tell he didn't buy her mother's story. At least, she thought she could tell he didn't buy it.

The truth was, she didn't trust anything she thought or felt anymore. The little doctor at the hospital had said she was psychiatrically sick—which meant crazy. How could a crazy girl know when she was right and when she was just being—crazy?

Ron was still staring at her with that funny expression in his eyes. And suddenly she was sure he knew all about her—and what she did. He could tell just by looking at her. Because in the hospital she'd changed; she'd become a person who could no longer keep her secrets. Now it was like there was a sign on her telling the whole world about the ugly, disgusting things she did. And it would be that way forever. Wherever she went people would always know about her.

A part of her brain said she was being crazy to think this way. But then, she was crazy. Crazy, nuts, loony tunes, wacko, psychiatrically sick; they're all words that mean me, she thought. And she ducked her head so Ron couldn't see into her eyes.

She wanted to run. She wanted to get out of the rink and run until she found a dark, safe place where she could curl up and hide. It took all her powers of concentration to stand still while Ron turned his look from her to her mom and they set up the next week's schedule.

21

At first it seemed as if her house was going to be her safe hiding place. Katherine took her back there and then left for work. After her mother was gone, Katie wandered around her home, luxuriating in the unfamiliar sensation of having nothing to do and no one to answer to. But then the novelty began to wear off. Katie realized she'd never been home by herself without Katherine before—at least, not for any length of time. Her mother was always there, filling it with her sounds; with orders, demands, tirades, or even just the clicking of her high heels on the wooden floors. Without her the place seemed huge. And too quiet.

Katie walked to the kitchen and back to the living room. Now she was moving aimlessly because she couldn't bear to be still. It began to dawn on her that she'd never been alone like this anywhere. There had always been coaches and teachers around her. There were always homework assignments to finish, or new skating moves to learn. But now there was no one. And there was nothing for her to do.

She went back into the kitchen and poured herself a glass of water. The clock above the sink said ten-fifteen. She couldn't believe so little time had passed. She checked her watch—the clock was right. It was scary how slowly the day was going. She was used to a schedule that was so packed that she had never had a minute to waste. Now suddenly there were long, horrible hours stretching ahead of her with nothing to fill them except her own crazy thoughts.

As if on cue, the words "psychiatrically sick" floated into

her mind. She tried to push them away but they came back. "You're going to get psychiatrically sicker," the doctor had said.

"I'm not going to think about it," she told herself.

She walked back into the living room, sat down on the couch, and turned on the TV. When the other kids talked about the soaps and talk shows they'd watched during vacations, she'd always been envious. Now this was her chance to waste a whole day in front of the tube like everybody else.

But the talk show she selected couldn't compete with the fears that were building inside her. What did it mean to be psychiatrically sick? Would she wind up dirty and homeless, talking to herself on the street? Would they put her in a hospital? For how long? What happened to people in there? What if she had to stay for the rest of her life?

"Stop thinking like this," the voice in her head commanded, but the fears wouldn't go away. Was this sickness going to take over her mind until she couldn't think? What did you do if you couldn't think? How did you live? "Stop this," the voice in her head shouted. But another voice insisted, "What do you do if you're crazy? How do you live?"

Something was hurting her. She looked down to see that she had clasped her hands together so tightly that her fingers were digging painfully into the swollen flesh of the injured hand. Even under the thick gauze wrapping the area around the cut, it was bulging with the pressure. Slowly she released her hands. But the bandage held her attention. It was so very white and clean. She began to pick at the adhesive tape with her fingernail . . .

She stopped herself and put her hand under one of the sofa cushions to get it out of her sight. "You hurt yourself out of an emotional need," the doctor at the hospital had said. That was what made her crazy—hurting herself. So if she took off the bandage and did what she wanted to do to the cut, she was psychiatrically sick.

Besides, this compulsion was something new. It was the first time she'd ever thought about reopening a wound. She had a feeling it would hurt even worse than cutting. So that would mean she was even sicker than Dr. Karachi thought. Also, she wasn't spacing out. This was more like the time she cut her breast; it was just something she wanted to do. Suddenly, these questions all seemed very important as she sat alone in the empty house. And they seemed very scary. "But if I don't touch the bandage or the cut, then I'm all right," she told herself. "If I don't touch them, and I don't make any new cuts, I'm not really crazy. Okay?" She realized she was making a bargain with someone—but she wasn't sure who. Her teeth started chattering with the cold. "Please don't let me be crazy," she prayed to whoever it was, "please."

FOR THREE LONG days she managed to keep herself from pulling off the bandage. For three days she battled the temptation to cut herself and kept her scissors in her tote bag. At times the urge to comfort herself with them was so strong the only way she could escape was to sleep. There were times when her need was so great she couldn't even do that. Then she paced around the rug in the living room in ever decreasing circles. It was hard all the time, but the worst was the late afternoon, as the sun was sinking, right before Katherine came home.

The fight took all of her time and energy. No way she could do homework, or even read her beloved Dorothy Parker for fun. She was glad she didn't have to skate because there was no way she could have concentrated. At least a dozen times a day, she told herself it wasn't worth it. Once she actually peeled most of the tape off her bandage. But the fear of being sick was stronger than her need, so she stuck the tape back on again. And went back to her lonely battle.

She was waiting for the urge to disappear. It never did, but as the days went by, and she refused to give in, she started feeling a weird kind of pride in herself. This was a victory— it was as big a win as any she'd ever had on the ice or in school. She was proving she wasn't sick, proving she was in control. She felt powerful. She was pleased with herself.

Then, on the third day, the phone call came from the school.

22

Actually, there were two phone calls. They came in the evening, after Katherine was home from work. The first was from the school secretary. Katie could tell it was someone from the school just from the look on her mother's face.

"Well, you can tell Dr. Kendall that my daughter is not going to see any goddamned shrink," Katherine shouted and hung up. But a few minutes later Dr. Kendall himself called.

At first her mom tried shouting at him, but before long she was listening—angrily but silently. When he started talking, Katherine's face flushed to a dark, angry red. Katie watched in fascination as the color gradually faded until she looked white and pinched.

Finally she said, "Well, I don't have any choice, do I?" and hung up. Obviously, she'd lost her fight. Knowing how her mom felt about losing, Katie braced herself for the explosion of fury and recriminations that had to come. She knew Katherine would aim it all at her. Her mother already blamed her for jeopardizing their dream; this most recent humiliation was just the icing on the cake.

But the explosion did not come. After she hung up, Katherine moved slowly and wearily to the kitchen table, where she sat for a long time staring into space. Katie waited until she couldn't stand it anymore.

"Mom," she said nervously, "what did they say? What do I have to do?"

Her mother pulled herself to her feet. "Make dinner for yourself," she said in a dull voice. "I have a headache; I'm going to bed." Then, with a heavy step Katie had never seen before, she walked out of the kitchen.

For a moment shock outweighed every other feeling for Katie. The idea of Katherine, who was never tired or sick, taking to her bed before dinner was unthinkable. Nothing stopped her mother. Nothing made her move slowly like the stranger who was making her way down the hall at that moment. From the back she even looked shorter. Katie realized that was because Katherine, who prided herself on her perfect posture, was slumping.

"Mom, please," she called to the retreating figure. "Tell me what they're going to make me do." The only answer she got was the sound of Katherine's door slamming.

And she was all alone in the house again.

The silence was horrible—it told her louder than words that this was all her fault. If she hadn't gone nuts in the hallway at school, Dr. Kendall wouldn't be demanding that she see a shrink. Then her mother wouldn't have been fighting with him. And she wouldn't have lost the fight. Katie had caused her mother's defeat. And now Katherine's door was closed. And Katherine was behind it, refusing to talk. The silence was growing in the house. It seemed to fill all the rooms. Soon it would start sucking out the air, making it impossible to breathe.

Katie looked at the closed door. She wanted to bang on it so hard she would force Katherine to come out. She wanted to scream that her mother couldn't do this to her. She wanted to beg her mother to forgive her. "I'm sorry, Mom," she whispered. "Please don't be mad at me. I'm so sorry." But Katherine didn't hear her. And the door didn't open. And the silence was still growing. There was only one thing to do. Her tote bag was in the living room; she went to get it. A part of her wanted to protest, she'd fought so hard not to do this; but there was no way to stop. She picked up the purse and moved back to the kitchen, where the light was good. She sat in the same chair Katherine had used, and put her bandaged hand on the table. For three long days she'd resisted touching her hand; for three long days she'd won her battle. Now she started to cry—not with sounds, but with tears that filled her eyes, blurring her vision and making it hard to see the adhesive tape on the bandage. But she found it and pulled at it until it gave way. Then she unwrapped the white gauze. The tears were running down her cheeks now as she leaned over to look at her hand.

The swelling had gone down, but the jagged cut hadn't healed yet. It still zigzagged across the back of her hand, covered by a reddish brown scab. The three butterfly tapes held it together. She looked down at them; the edge of the middle one was starting to curl back. She picked at it with her thumbnail until she could get enough of it loose to pull. Slowly and deliberately, she ripped the tape off the wound. It reopened and started to bleed. She pulled the two other tapes off. Tears slowly rolled down her cheeks. She took her scissors out of her purse and finished what she'd started.

LATER THAT NIGHT, after the bleeding had stopped, she lay in her bed, unable to sleep. Her shiny new victory was gone. And now she realized how powerless she truly was. She'd rewrapped her hand, so the new wound was hidden. No one ever had to know what she'd done. But she knew. The doctor at the hospital was right. She was crazy. And she was very frightened.

THE NEXT MORNING Katherine told her in a few terse sentences that she was going to have an appointment with Ms. Santiago.

"There's no way out," Katherine said. "The damn school has me over a barrel, thanks to you and your temper tantrum. They'll pull your scholarship if you don't see their psychologist." Katie nodded numbly, too worn out by the battle she'd lost the night before to fight anymore.

23

Ms. Santiago's office was in an enormous medical complex near Westchester Academy. It was an ugly, ugly place, Katie thought as she saw four gray high-rise buildings surrounding a multilevel parking lot.

Katherine drove past the parking lot entrance and pulled up in front of the main doors of the complex. She stopped the car.

"Well, get out," she said.

"Aren't you coming in with me?" Katie asked in a voice that sounded, even to her, small.

"I have to get back to work."

Katie fiddled nervously with the door handle. "I don't know how long this is supposed to take," she said. "Should I call you at the bank when I'm through?"

Katherine shrugged. "I can't come get you until my lunch hour. So find a place to read or something." Katie nodded, but she couldn't make herself open the car door. Katherine turned to look at her. "Katie, you have to do this," she said. "Just stay strong and don't let her push you around. And remember, you don't have to tell her things that are none of her business. Now get going, you don't want to be late." Katie nodded again and got out of the car. Katherine drove off quickly.

The doors of the main building were large and made of glass. There were ramps for wheelchairs next to the stairs leading into the building. Clearly, this was a place where sick people came. And now she was one of them.

— ❊ —

Ms. Santiago's waiting room contrasted pleasantly with the gray-on-gray drabness of the rest of the building. The walls in her waiting room were painted a pale peach; the sofa was covered with a flowered fabric of peach, cream, and light green. Even the tissues in the box on the coffee table were a pinky peach color.

Katie pulled a copy of *Vogue* out of a wicker magazine rack and tried to read, but her mind was racing back and forth between fear of what was going to happen next and something else that she dimly recognized as a tiny spark of hope.

The doctor at the hospital had said she had to get help. Katie wasn't sure exactly what that might entail, but she did know she was out of control in a way that was getting very scary. As she looked at the single print of a lady in a Victorian dress on the wall of the waiting room, she reminded herself that the teachers and staff at the academy had always been good to her—so maybe, hopefully, they were getting her the help she needed when they set up this appointment with Ms. Santiago.

As for Ms. Santiago herself, Katie didn't know much about her except that she always looked pretty and she seemed friendly. Several of the kids at school who had had dealings with her said they liked her. So maybe she really could help cure the psychiatric sickness. All Katie knew for sure was that she couldn't fight it on her own.

Ms. Santiago opened the door to her office. "Come in, Katie," she said. Katie stood, her heart pounding hard.

"Please don't let anything bad happen," she prayed as she walked across what felt like miles of peach-colored carpet to the doorway.

Ms. Santiago's office was a peach, cream, and green extension of her waiting room. "You can sit there," she said. Her voice seemed warm enough. She indicated an over-stuffed couch.

"This is a very pretty room," Katie said. She always tried to compliment adults on something they owned or did. There was no quiver in her voice when she spoke and that pleased her. "I like the colors. My mom made me a costume once that was peach and cream. I won my first competition in it." It never hurt to remind anyone from Westchester Academy that she was their skating champion.

But she might as well have saved her breath. Because Ms. Santiago was too busy looking at Katie's injured hand to pay attention to what she was saying. The cut had bled slightly through the gauze wrapping during the night and Ms. Santiago stared at it for a second, then quickly averted her eyes. Katie could feel that she was revolted by the sight of it. The psychologist hadn't been in school when Katie flipped out, but she had to have learned about it. And obviously, she was disgusted by what she'd heard. *I wonder how horrified you'd have been if you'd seen me with my scissors last night,* Katie thought.

Ms. Santiago seemed to realize she'd been giving herself away because she shrugged her shoulders quickly and smiled in Katie's direction. But she avoided making eye contact. Katie sank deeper into the puffy, pretty couch. Suddenly she felt as if she weren't quite clean—as if she didn't belong in this perfect pastel room with perfect Ms. Santiago.

"So, Katie," said Ms. Santiago, "I'm sure you have some idea why you're here." She gazed at an arrangement of silk flowers in a moss basket. Katie stared at it too—and said nothing.

"There's nothing to be afraid of," said Ms. Santiago in a tone that was probably meant to be reassuring but came out slightly irritated. Katie still didn't say anything. Finally, Ms. Santiago had to look directly at her.

I won that round, Katie thought to herself.

"The school has some real concerns about you, Katie," Ms. Santiago said. "I do, as well. We want to help you, but first you have to help us." She picked up a pad and pen. Obviously she was planning to take notes—like the two doctors at the hospital. What was with these people? It was as if Katie were some kind of chem lab experiment that hadn't worked out right, and the only way they could salvage their grade was to write a great report. Still, the word "help" had been used. The hope that had been dying inside her came back very faintly. "What kind of help do you want to give me?" Katie asked warily.

"I'm going to recommend a good therapist for you."

"Aren't you a therapist?"

"Yes, but I won't be treating you. That wouldn't be ethical because I work for your school."

And besides, you'd rather be dead than get involved with me, Katie thought.

"That'll teach you," the voice inside her head sneered at her. "As soon as people know about you, they run. And that's the way it's always going to be."

She felt something dark and heavy cover her like a blanket.

"We know from your hospital report that you have a history of hurting yourself," said Ms. Santiago. "I'd like you to tell me how long this behavior has been going on." She said the word "behavior" as if it were a dirty word. Katie looked at her feet and said nothing.

"How extensive is it? By that I mean, how many times a week on average do you cut yourself?"

Katie said nothing.

"Do you do other things—like burn yourself, or hit yourself?"

Do you really think I'd tell you if I did? Katie asked her silently.

"What triggered that incident at school earlier this week? Can you tell me why you went over the edge?"

Katie shook her head.

"What about drugs or alcohol, ever do any experimenting?"

Katie shook her head again. Her silence was exasperating Ms. Santiago, although the woman was trying hard to hide it. It was kind of fun to watch her. After a lifetime of trying to please adults, Katie was enjoying deliberately making one angry.

But Ms. Santiago smiled as if nothing were wrong. "Well, I think that's enough for now," she said as if Katie had been cooperating all along.

Katie looked at her, startled. "You mean we're through?" she asked. Ms. Santiago gave her a big, phony smile—the kind Katie herself often used when she wanted to put people off guard.

"Katie, let me share something with you," she said pleasantly. "I don't believe in coddling people. If you've decided to stonewall me, that's fine. I accept your choice. But if you expect me to beg you to talk, you've got the wrong person. I'm not going to waste my time and energy trying to drag answers out of you." She made her hands into a little tent with her long fingernails touching. "Now, I'm going to share something else with you. I think you have some serious problems. The form of psychosis you present can escalate with time. In extreme cases, women have been known to seriously injure or even disfigure themselves," she added with what Katie would have sworn was a little shiver. "The fascination with blood and pain can become consuming to the point that full-time hospitalization is required.

"You're a pretty girl," Ms. Santiago went on. "I would have done anything to look like you at your age. You have talent, you're bright, you have everything going for you. So get it together." She got up and opened her office door. "I'm going to recommend a therapist for you. His name is Dr. Sherman. If he has the time to take you on, work with him. Don't be foolish, Katie." She smiled. The session was over.

AS SHE WAITED for the elevator to take her back down to the lobby, Katie paced, too angry to stand still. She couldn't believe it. Was this what she'd been so afraid of—and so hopeful about? This big, fat nothing? She'd gone through twelve hours of misery because of this; her mom had fought with the school and lost. And for what? A stupid meeting that had accomplished absolutely nothing. She hated Ms. Santiago. She hated Dr. Kendall and Ms. Moran and all the other adults who said they wanted to help when they had nothing to offer. Most of all, she hated herself, because for a few minutes she'd actually allowed herself to believe in them.

But they'd never trick her like that again. She'd never trust any of them. And that included the latest therapist Ms. Santiago was going to recommend—this Dr. Sherman.

24

Sandy Sherman looked over Katie Roskova's report, which Ilene Santiago had sent to him.

"It's a self-mutilation case. The girl's name is Katie Roskova, and she's not going to be easy," Ilene had warned after he'd agreed to see the girl.

"The interesting ones usually aren't," he'd answered.

"If that's how you feel, then this kid will fascinate you," she'd said, then added, "Sooner you than me, Sandy."

Sandy shook his head at the memory. He liked Ilene well enough as a person, but she was the kind of therapist he'd never understand. She avoided the difficult cases he found so exciting. Her private practice catered to the upscale and mildly neurotic, and even though she was on staff at a private school, the bulk of her patients were adults.

Sandy preferred kids. With a few exceptions, he'd found that under the attitude and bravado, most of them had a vulnerability that touched him. They were passionate, and innocent—for all their surface knowledge—and sometimes they were wise. And they never, ever bored him. His wife, who was also a therapist and knew about the occupational hazards of their profession, said he wanted to save them. "You've got to watch that therapist-as-white-knight complex," she said. If she was right—and she usually was when it came to him—he'd live with it. One of the good things about being fifty years old was that you started accepting yourself. Or at least you tried to.

As for the rough cases, he liked them too. He'd begun treating anorexics and bulimics back in the days when the common wisdom was that these kids were doomed to die. He had refused to believe it, and he now had a list of success stories to prove he'd been right. He was proud of that track record—and if it was arrogant of him, well, he'd live with that too.

And now, if his first visit with her went as expected, he'd be treating Katie Roskova.

According to the hospital report, there were scars on her arms, which indicated that she'd been cutting herself for some time. But Ilene said no one at the school had had a clue that anything was wrong. While it was true that there were no exact profiles for kids with psychiatric problems, the warning signs that said a child was in trouble were usually hard to miss. Most of the time you were looking at a loner, a kid who was isolated and secretive. Performance in class was usually well below normal. Often there was a lack of personal hygiene. For self-mutilators, there were certain commonsense signals as well—long sleeves that were worn even in the hottest weather to hide scars, or a hat pulled down to cover bald spots because some of these kids pulled out their hair—that kind of thing, coupled with the other signs of disturbance, should be a red flag to teachers and school staff.

But Katie Roskova had been a school star. For years she'd presented the picture of a girl who was successful and outgoing. Obviously, she was clever and resourceful at covering up her disease. She'd also managed to evade answering Ilene Santiago's questions in the evaluation session.

As for Katie's support team, which was the way he liked to think of the family in these instances, there didn't seem to be much help there. Katie had a driven mother who opposed therapy for her child. The father was even less of a potential ally. According to Ilene, it was known that Mr. Roskova was alive, but there had never been an actual sighting of him by anyone connected with the school. He'd moved out of state after his divorce from Katie's mother. It seemed safe to assume that his interest in his daughter was, at best, limited. Katie had no siblings. Sandy closed the file thoughtfully. Ilene was right, he decided. Katie Roskova wouldn't be an easy case.

25

As her mother drove her to her appointment with Dr. Sherman, Katie told herself there was nothing to be scared of. Because now she knew what to expect. This Sandy Sherman wouldn't be any different from the doctors at the hospital or Ms. Santiago. He'd start out with a speech about how sick she was and how much he wanted to help her. But he wouldn't mean it. While he talked to her, he'd play with a clipboard or at least write notes so he wouldn't have to look at her. He'd pretend he wasn't disgusted by her, but it would be written all over his face that he was. Finally, he'd ask a lot of dumb questions, and when she wouldn't answer him, he'd tell her there was nothing he could do for her if she refused to cooperate. Eventually, he'd ask her to leave his office and not come back. Secretly, he'd be glad to have an excuse to get rid of her. End of story.

Katherine stopped the car in front of Dr. Sherman's office building to let her out. This time Katie didn't even bother to ask if her mother was staying. Dr. Sherman's office building was actually an elderly Victorian house in one of the older neighborhoods near the train station. A few years before in the area, several abandoned houses that were falling apart had been renovated for commercial use. Katie had to admit that they were pretty, with their gables and turrets and front porches loaded with ornate wooden trim. There seemed to be several doctors' offices in the building. Dr. Sherman's was on the third floor in the front and she had to climb a wide, curved staircase to get to it.

His waiting room was nothing at all like Ms. Santiago's. Hers had been spacious and picture-perfect; his was small and kind of crowded. There was a water cooler in one corner, and several chairs clustered around a small couch. Everything seemed to be in shades of brown and gold except the walls, which were off-white. Nothing really matched, but there were lots of pictures on the walls, which made the place feel cozy.

Before she had a chance to sit down, the office door opened and a man came out. His hair was white and a short white beard covered his chin. He had brown eyes. Katie thought he was about six feet tall, although she wasn't much good at estimating people's heights. His clothes seemed awfully casual for a doctor—he wore a brown sweater and blue jeans. He smiled and said, "Hi, Katie. Come on in. I'm Sandy Sherman. Most of my patients call me Sandy, but you do whatever makes you comfortable." He led her into a room with three straight walls and one that curved out over the street. Sunshine poured in through five long windows. When you looked out it was like being in a tree house.

SANDY WATCHED the girl as she moved into his office. She was a pretty kid, conservatively dressed in a long-sleeved blouse, a pleated skirt, and a sweater vest. She carried herself gracefully and with confidence. Nothing in her body language suggested that she had a thing to hide. If it hadn't been for the bruises on her forehead and her bandaged hand, he would have found it hard to believe she was the girl described in the hospital report. He watched her look around his office, her face brightening briefly when she saw the trees outside his windows. Well, that gave them something in common, he thought; he liked them too.

"It's a great view, isn't it?" he said. "This office is in the turret of the house. That's why I decided to take the space. I like having windows all around me." She nodded politely. It didn't seem to bother her that he'd picked up on her reaction. This kid was used to being watched.

Katie was aware that the doctor was watching her, but that was okay, because she knew she could handle him. When he started asking questions, she'd give him the silent treatment just the way she'd given it to Ms. Santiago. In the meantime she continued to study the room. It wasn't large; there was a desk in one corner, and shelves and filing cabinets lined one portion of the wall. There was a green couch with lots of pillows against the opposite wall, and two gray chairs were facing it. There were more pillows on the chairs. Dr. Sherman sat in one of them and waited for her to settle. She perched on the couch. He smiled at her again, leaned forward, and picked up a pile of papers. Predictable, she thought, next he'd start with the dumb questions. Well, she was ready for him.

As he picked up his notes, Sandy saw a flicker of something almost like satisfaction cross Katie's face. On instinct, he put the notes down and leaned back in his chair. Easy does it, he thought. He wanted to get through to this kid right up front, before she had a chance to write him off. She'd been conning adults most of her life, avoiding them and neutralizing them. She needed to know it wasn't going to be quite so easy to get rid of him.

Katie was confused. At this point this Dr. Sherman person was supposed to hide his face in his notes and start with the questions. Instead, he was leaning back in his chair as if he had all the time in the world and they were just going to have a friendly little chat. Everything about him seemed to say he was prepared to like her. For a second she wondered if he would. Then she reminded herself not to be stupid. Once he got to know her, he'd be like everybody else.

"When do you go back to the hospital to get your hand checked?" he asked so suddenly she forgot all about not answering him and said, "Next Wednesday."

"Does it still hurt?" he asked.

"No," she said. But she was lying; it had been hurting ever since she'd reopened the wound.

"The only reason I asked was, it looks to me as if someone took off that bandage," he said. "If the cut has been opened again, you might want to have a doctor look at it so it doesn't get infected."

She'd been afraid it was getting infected. It was almost as if he knew what she'd done. But if he did, he didn't seem revolted or disgusted by it. In fact, he was calm and kind of friendly—as if they were having a talk about something that interested him a lot, but it wasn't personal. It was a very weird response. It unnerved her, and she didn't like it.

The good news, Sandy thought, was that he'd gotten her attention. But now he'd better back off before he became the enemy.

"Katie, I've read the report from the hospital," he said gently. "So I know about your scars, I know what you do, and I know what it means. At least, I do in clinical terms. I don't know what it means to you specifically. I'm counting on you to tell me that. Would you? Could we start by talking about your history? Perhaps you could tell me how long you've been doing this?"

She felt a little lurch of relief. He was finally asking questions. This was what she had expected. She knew how to deal with him now. She looked at the floor and said nothing.

Sandy realized he'd made a mistake. She was going to shut down on him. Or at least that was what she thought she was going to do.

"Okay," he said mildly. "You don't want to talk about it. I figured you might not. I just thought I'd give it a shot."

She sneaked a quick look up at him. Good, he thought. You haven't tuned me out completely. Not yet.

"But we can't sit here and stare at each other for the next forty-five minutes," he went on. "That would be kind of dumb. So I guess I have to tell you what I know about what you do. Feel free to jump in anytime."

Normally he tried to avoid doing the talking during a ses-

sion, but he couldn't let her set the rules. She was determined that they wouldn't talk; he had to let her know that
they would.

"First, let's give what you do a name," he said. "In technical terms it's called self-mutilation. What it really is, is a coping mechanism. You have a lot of feelings you can't handle.
You may not even be able to identify them. But they make
you very anxious, and in some way that you'll probably have
to explain to me, inflicting pain on yourself makes the anxiety go away. How am I doing so far?"

She wanted to tell him that what he was doing was making her mad. He was being so smiley and cute about trying to
trick her into talking. Meanwhile, he sat in his chair telling
her about herself as if she were some sort of case history in
a book.

"What you've done," he went on in his chatty way, "is sub-
stitute physical pain for psychological pain. When you hurt
yourself, that focuses your mind on the blood you produce
and the physical sensations you feel instead of the emotions
you can't handle. It's an ingenious solution to a problem that
must seem impossible. I admire you for coming up with it,
Katie."

He sounded so genuine, she shot another look at him. His
expression was sincere too.

"Don't trust him," warned the voice inside her head.

"And I want you to know that I'd never ask you to stop
using your method of coping while you still need it," he
said.

She wanted to laugh in his face at that one. Except that
she was too angry. Was he trying to tell her he'd let her go on
using her scissors? Was she supposed to believe that would
be okay with him? What kind of an idiot did he take her for?
She almost asked him, but then she swallowed the question.
But not before he saw what she was thinking.

"Why does that make you so angry, Katie?" he asked
sharply.

"It doesn't."

"Sure it does. I can see it in your face. Why? What's wrong with what I just said?"

"I don't believe you," she blurted out.

"What don't you believe?"

"That you'd let me . . ." she stopped short.

"That I'd let you hurt yourself?" he asked gently. She didn't answer, but suddenly, against her will, her eyes started filling with tears. Which was all his fault and she hated him for it. But she couldn't stop listening to him.

Don't notice the tears, Sandy told himself. Don't offer her a tissue or ask her what's going on. Just keep talking.

"You're right," he said. "I don't want you hurting yourself. My goal is for you to stop that. Eventually. But not until you're ready. Which means we have to give you some other ways of dealing with your problems.

"You see, I want to teach you how to get in touch with all those emotions that are making you feel out of control. We'll put labels on them so you can talk about them. In fact, we may invent a whole new vocabulary for you to talk about your feelings. You may not want to say the word 'anger,' you might want to call it 'spinach.' That's okay with me as long as we find a way to say what's going on. Because once you can say it, you can handle it. Without slamming your hand in a locker door or cutting your arm."

She'd stopped crying now. She was looking at him, paying attention against her will. He'd have to shut up soon or he'd lose her, but he still had another point to make.

"After we've helped you find the skills to cope, you'll have to decide if you want to stop hurting yourself," he said. "It'll be your choice. But I think you'll want to." He paused, then added softly, "Because I think you're already a little worried about yourself, Katie."

The nod of her head was so slight he almost missed it.

"It doesn't have to be that way," he said. "I believe that. And if you and I work together, you'll have to start believing it too. I know your school says you have to see me and that's why you're here. And that's all right for now. But I'd like to know you're keeping an open mind."

This time there was no nod. She'd heard enough for one day; it was time to wind up.

"What do you say?" he asked lightly. "Want to give me and my ideas a try?" She hesitated. "Look at it this way, what do you have to lose?"

For a long time she didn't say anything. Then finally, her eyes still on her feet, she asked, "What do we do next?"

"You come and see me once a week. We talk. As soon as we can arrange it, I'll want to have a family session with you and your mother and father all together."

She gave him a cynical little smile. "You'll never get my dad," she said. "Not if he has to be in the same room with my mom."

"How much do you want to bet?"

For the first time during the session, she giggled.

THE SESSION WAS drawing to a close. There was one practical thing he could do for her before she left. He scribbled a note on a piece of paper. "If you'd rather not wait until Wednesday to have that hand looked at, Dr. Bernstien on the second floor is a friend of mine; he'll take care of it for you," he said. He held out the note to her. She looked at it for a second, then took it without saying a word.

AFTER KATIE WAS gone, Sandy wrote up his report on the session. When he'd first started as a therapist, he'd been very strict about keeping a detailed account of each patient's progress, which he wrote using proper terminology. But you got over that sort of thing once you had a little more mileage on you. Now his reports were more like notes to himself written in his own personal shorthand.

As usual in this stage of the game, he wasn't sure exactly what he'd accomplished with Katie Roskova in their first encounter. He knew the girl had said more to him than she'd planned to . . . but he'd talked even more than she had. How much of what he'd said had she heard? If she'd heard any of it. More important, had he managed to establish the beginning of the trust they'd have to have if they were to work together? She was a hard kid to read. He didn't even know if she'd trusted him enough to see Howard Bernstien on her way out of the building.

He pondered for a few seconds before he finally jotted down the one positive note he felt he could take away from the meeting. "Deep down, Katie knows she's in trouble," he wrote. It was a start.

26

Katie's hand was still stinging from the cleaning Dr. Bernstien had given it. It *had* been infected, although he had assured her that it hadn't gotten too bad. She admitted to herself grudgingly that she owed Dr. Sherman for suggesting that his pal take care of it. Not that she had any intention of letting him know that. As she walked out of the old Victorian house, she wondered why she felt that way. Normally she would have been delighted to tell an adult how grateful she was for something he'd done. Adults loved that stuff. But somehow she didn't want to flatter Dr. Sherman. Maybe because it would be so disappointing if he fell for it.

SHE WAS SO involved in her own thoughts she didn't even see her mom waiting for her in the car in front of the house. Katherine had to blow the horn to get her attention.

"Well, what did this Dr. Sherman have to say?" Katherine demanded as soon as Katie was in the car. Katie looked over at her. Her mom was staring straight ahead. She was holding the steering wheel so tightly her hands were white around the knuckles. She's really upset about this, Katie thought.

"He asked some dumb questions," Katie said. Katherine seemed to tighten even more.

"What did you say?" she asked.

Katie shrugged. "Not much of anything." She stole another quick glance at the rigid figure sitting next to her. "It's no big deal, Mom," she said. "A lot of skaters have shrinks."

"But this is different."

"Not really. He did a lot of talking about managing my feelings better."

"What feelings?"

"Who knows? I didn't really listen to him."

"And you didn't say anything?"

"I didn't have to. He did most of the talking. He likes the sound of his own voice."

The half-truths seemed to relax Katherine a little. She loosened her death grip on the wheel and sat silently for a long time. "What's he like?" she asked at last.

"I don't know . . . He's an older guy. Sort of like a teacher."

She watched her mother gather herself together. Obviously, her next question was going to be hard for her to ask.

"What did you think of him? Did you like him?"

Something made her say, "No." Even though she wasn't sure it was true.

That seemed to satisfy her mother, and Katherine smiled slightly as she started the car. Katie leaned back and closed her eyes; it wasn't as though she'd lied to her mom, she reasoned—not really. She'd just tried to make Katherine feel a little easier about things. Otherwise she'd never stop quizzing Katie. The last thing Katie wanted to do was talk with her mother about her session with Sandy Sherman.

She'd just started to drift off when she felt the car turn off the main road, drive a few feet, and stop. She opened her eyes to see that they were in a small shopping center a couple of miles from their house.

"Come on," said Katherine, "we're going to have some fun." She got out of the car and led the way to a popular local sandwich shop.

"A hot fudge sundae for me," she announced gaily to the waitress. "Caramel nut for you, Katie?" A little dazed, Katie nodded. Caramel nut sundaes were her absolute favorite, but they were strictly forbidden when you had to watch your weight as carefully as she did.

"Mom, my diet . . ." she began.

"Just this once," said Katherine. "After the way you handled that shrink, you deserve a treat."

The sundaes came and they both attacked them greedily, spooning up mouthfuls of cold, sweet ice cream and hot, gooey sauce. Katherine made a game of eating the ice cream out from under her maraschino cherry, which finally settled into the dregs of the hot fudge with a satisfying plop. Katie laughed and got a dribble of caramel on her chin that Katherine wiped away and then licked clean from her finger.

If only it could always be like this, Katie thought. But she didn't say it out loud.

"That was good," Katherine said when the last drops of sauce had been scraped off the sides of the dishes. Katie nodded enthusiastically.

"I used to love hot fudge sundaes when I was a kid," Katherine went on. "There was a place right near Gregson's rink that made the best. They used real whipped cream and gave you all the chopped nuts you wanted." For a moment she was lost in the memory, then she came back to the present. "You'll have to see this shrink for a while," she said briskly. "Play up to him, because he's going to be giving the school a report on you, and a good one will get them off our backs. It's too bad we have to waste our time on this, but it can't be helped. I'll tell Ron you'll be missing practice one day a week for a while. You just find a way to keep that shrink happy without letting him get to you."

Katie nodded solemnly. Privately, she was wondering how happy Katherine was going to be when she found out she had to attend a family session. With her ex-husband, no less.

27

Katie didn't have much time to worry about the session Dr. Sherman wanted to have with her father and mother. She doubted he could make it happen, but that was his problem. Meanwhile, she had troubles of her own. It was time for her to go back to school. The deal with the academy had been that they'd let her come back as soon as she was seeing a therapist. The visit with Dr. Sherman fulfilled that requirement, so her enforced school vacation was over.

She'd already started skating again. Ron had taken the news about her missing the weekly practice session surprisingly well. He didn't ask why it had to happen, and he didn't even mention that the championships were a few months away. Except for the fact that she was a little rusty after her days off, getting back in the old skating routine had been easy.

BUT GOING BACK to Westchester Academy was something else. She had to face a school full of kids who had last seen her screaming and banging her head against a wall. She spent a couple of sleepless nights wondering how she was going to pull it off.

Finally, the only game plan she could come up with was to tough it out. She slipped into the school the way she always did. But then, instead of smiling and saying hi to people, she walked as fast as she could to her first class, being careful not to make eye contact with anyone along the way. She lugged all of her books for all of her classes because she couldn't, she wouldn't, let anyone see her going near her locker. Fearing Ms. Moran might say something about her recent absence from school, Katie skipped her English class and hid in the girls' room. At lunchtime, she left the building and hung out in the parking lot so she wouldn't have to try to find someone to eat with. Still, she was sure she was getting weird looks, snickers, and whispers behind her back. At least, she thought she was sure. That was what made the whole thing so difficult; she didn't know if she was imagining the slights and insults or if they were real. If she'd only had a couple of close friends, they could have given her a reality check. But she'd never had friends like that. So she walked down the halls daring anyone to say anything to her. And feeling like crying because she was so alone.

JENNY MORAN watched Katie make her lonely way through the halls on her first day back and felt her heart ache for the child.

"But I don't know what I can do for her," she said to Ilene and Barbara when she went to their office during her free period. "It's obvious Katie doesn't want any help from me. I think she cut my class this morning to avoid me."

"She's embarrassed," said Barbara. "Maybe you can take her aside quietly and have a talk with her."

"No," said Ilene. "Leave it alone, Jenny. I've placed her with a really fine therapist. He seems to have a flair for working with teenagers—especially girls with self-esteem issues. Now it's up to them to work this out together. It really isn't appropriate, at this point, for you to get involved."

As usual, Ilene made Jenny feel totally inadequate. Maybe it was the jargon she used. Or her impersonal tone of voice.

"Got it," Jenny said and started to leave. But then she remembered what had happened the last time she'd been worried about Katie and she'd allowed Ilene to scare her off. "Ilene," she said, "what's the man's name? The one who's treating Katie?"

On her way back to her classroom, she stopped off at the main office to use the phone book. She looked up Dr. Sherman's telephone number and wrote it in her address book. Just in case.

THE FIRST LONG day was finally over. Katie was about to escape from the school building when she heard someone call out, "Hey, you leaving already?" At first she wasn't sure the words were directed at her. But when she hesitated, the voice said, "Yeah, I'm talking to you. How come you don't hang out by the gym anymore?" She whirled around to see Dave Malloy and two of his buddies grinning at her. Dave's sidekicks were jocks like him; one was named Josh, and she didn't know the third except by his reputation. Which was as bad as Dave's. All three of them stared at her.

"That was some show you put on last week," Dave said. Josh and the other guy chuckled. She felt herself blush. She wanted to sink through the floor, but she knew she'd never be that lucky.

"Tell me something," Dave went on. She had a feeling the other two knew what he was going to say and were egging him on. If she could have run away she would have, but her feet wouldn't move. All she could do was stay frozen where she was and wait for whatever was coming. It came fast. "Did you finally get over your PMS?" asked Dave.

It was humiliating to have a boy mention something so personal in that way. And she knew he knew it. If she could have thought of something to say—some quick comeback that was cool and maybe even a little funny—she could have turned the situation around. She might even have won his respect. But she stood there with her face getting redder and redder while the three boys laughed. Finally, her feet unglued themselves from the floor and she ran. The sound of their laughter followed her.

Later in the car on her way to the rink she realized Dave Malloy was the only person who'd spoken to her all day.

28

It took Sandy three weeks to get Katie's parents to agree to a joint family session. Oddly, the father was the easier one to convince.

"If you can get Katherine to tell the truth about our marriage, I'd pay to see it," he said on the phone. "Hell, I'll be glad to have an opportunity to set the record straight." Sandy restrained himself from pointing out that the upcoming meeting was supposed to be for his daughter's benefit.

Katherine Roskova was a tougher nut to crack. Only the threat of a bad report to the school finally brought her around.

He tried to address Katie's feelings about the meeting in her session.

"When was the last time you were in a room with both your parents, Katie?" he asked.

She appeared to think, then flashed him the big smile he had come to realize was one of her major weapons for avoiding him. "I don't remember," she said.

"How do you feel about it?"

"I never thought you'd get them together."

"But how do you feel about it?"

A flicker of irritation passed over her face. But she was still polite. "I think they'll handle it. I mean, they won't like it, but they'll be okay because they'll know it'll be over soon."

She had a gift for selective hearing. He tried a different tack. "Has this caused any problems for you at home?"

"Mom's not happy."

He'd bet she wasn't.

"But she'll be okay."

"You know, this is the kind of thing you could write down in that journal we talked about," he said. He'd suggested that she keep a diary, which they could read together during sessions. Sometimes writing down thoughts and feelings was a less dangerous first step than talking for very guarded kids. But so far she'd managed to sidestep the journal. Now she nodded politely. "I'll have to get a notebook real soon," she said.

For the next few minutes she'd managed to continue misunderstanding and not hearing him. Finally they'd chatted about ice-skating until it was time for her to leave.

ON THE DAY OF Katie's family session, Sandy found that he was unusually curious about meeting her parents. He had a few theories about the couple who had produced this bright, poised, sad little patient and he wanted to see how close on the money he was. They were due at three. He wondered who would arrive first. The front door intercom buzzed and he asked who it was.

"Pete Roskova," was the answer. Sandy pushed the button to let him in.

Peter Roskova was a slim, fine-boned man dressed in what Sandy, who had never actually read a copy of *GQ,* dimly recognized as the latest fashion for men. His hair was pulled back into a short, neat ponytail. He sported a small gold hoop in one ear. If he was feeling any apprehension about the session, it was well covered.

"Great idea putting professional offices in these old homes," he said, flashing a big smile. Okay, thought Sandy, now I know where Katie gets the charisma. The man toured the office, checking out the furniture and the pictures on the wall. "Nice," he said of the one expensively framed print. He sighed and looked around. "They don't make houses like they used to, do they?"

"You like old houses?" Sandy asked politely.

The smile vanished and was replaced by a look that could

only be described as cranky. "Who wouldn't? If you could see the place I live in now, you wouldn't ask. Of course I could never afford anything like this. Not on a restaurant manager's salary. Especially with the child support I have to cough up each month. Katherine and her lawyer broke my balls on that."

As if on cue, the buzzer went off again and Sandy opened the door to Katie and her mother.

Katherine Roskova seemed bigger than her former husband even though he had a couple of inches on her. Katie had her mother's striking coloring, huge eyes, and chiseled features. Her delicate build was from her father. As was her charm. There was nothing charming about Katherine Roskova. As she stormed into his office, her fury was like a physical presence she carried with her. Sandy felt himself pull back slightly. Peter all but flinched when she walked past him without saying a word.

Katherine and Katie sat together on the couch; Sandy and Peter each took a chair. Peter turned his body slightly so he was facing Sandy instead of his former wife and his daughter.

Sandy's focus was on Katie. The polite, controlled young lady was gone; in her place was a trapped child.

The silence in the room was overwhelming. Sandy let it ride. Suddenly Katie looked directly at him. There was great anger in her big, dark eyes. She wanted him to know it was directed at him.

"I HATE YOU," the voice inside Katie's head said to Sandy Sherman. "I hate you for this."

Her mom had stopped speaking to her again. "Look what you've done to me," Katherine had yelled after she'd been forced to agree to the family session. "Because you're crazy, I have to see a shrink. And that bastard will be there." Of course, "that bastard" was Katie's father.

And now Katie and her mom had to sit across from her dad because of Dr. Sandy I-just-want-to-help-you Sherman. Of course her father wouldn't look at her—he never did.

But, surprisingly, he started to speak.

"I've got to say, I'm not surprised that Katie's got psychological problems," he said to Sandy as if they were the only two people in the room.

"Why is that?" asked Sandy.

Her dad shrugged. "The way she's been raised. Her mother's certifiable." Katie could feel Katherine stiffen on the couch next to her, but she kept quiet.

"That's a pretty strong thing to say about someone," Dr. Sherman said calmly. "Could you be a little more specific? What are you talking about—exactly?"

"The goddamn skating," her father exploded. "Katherine was insane about Katie being a skater. Nothing else mattered. Every penny we had went into it. I wanted to start a business. I'm very good with computers. But we didn't have the money for me, it was all for lessons and costumes and the goddamn music arrangements. Do you think that's right?" he demanded.

Katie got the feeling that Dr. Sherman didn't want to answer that one. Serves you right, she thought. This was your big idea.

"I'm afraid I don't understand how that has an impact on Katie's present problems," Sandy Sherman said carefully.

"She's all over the poor kid. And I do mean all over. Get Katie to tell you what went on when her mother was teaching her to skate."

"I gave her the basis for what she has today!" Katherine cut in.

Well, Katie thought, there was no way her mom could have kept quiet for too long.

"I did everything for her," Katherine went on. "You say I was harsh . . ."

"Harsh! Jesus!"

"What have you ever done for her? What the hell have you ever done for anyone but yourself?"

"At least I'm not the one who drove her crazy."

Her father's words hurt. Katie told herself there was no reason for them to, but it didn't help. Tears came fast to her eyes and she had to blink them back.

"Mr. Roskova, there's something I don't get," Sandy said,

stepping in before her mom could go back at her dad and the war really started. "If you think your ex-wife is harming Katie, why aren't you trying to stop her?"

Her dad shot the therapist a resentful look. "There's nothing I can do," he said.

"Why?" asked Sandy.

"You don't know Katherine," said her father. "She took Katie over. She froze me out."

"You never wanted her," her mother shot back at him. Katie felt the tears come back; this time it was harder to blink them away.

"Look, Doctor, I tried to bring some sanity into our lives. But I just made it worse. Every time I tried to defend Katie, Katherine got even angrier."

"So you just left."

"It was the best thing for all of us." Her dad's voice was getting the high, whiny sound it got when he thought he was being criticized. "You don't know what my life was like when I was married to Katherine. All we did was fight. I knew I had to get out. I mean, it wasn't like it was helping Katie for me to stay there. After the divorce I tried to see Katie. But there was always something she had to do, like a class, or a skating meet, or all that homework for that private school she was in."

"And you had your new girlfriend," her mother shouted.

"Yes, all right. I got on with my life. I found a woman who loved me. I deserved some happiness, didn't I?" For the first time her dad faced her mom. "You can't stand that, can you? That I found someone who wanted to make me happy."

Katie's face was wet; there was no way she could blink back the tears now. Sandy Sherman got up and silently offered her a tissue box. The action stopped her parents cold. Katie started to sob. Her father's face got red; her mother had a strained, white look. Katie knew she was embarrassing both of them, but she couldn't help it.

"I've got to get out of here," her father muttered.

"Go ahead," said her mother. "It's what you always do when there's a problem."

Her father turned to Sandy. "You see?" he said. "This is

what always happens when I'm around. This is why I stay away."

"I'll take care of Katie," said her mother. "I always have. We don't need you."

"This is why I got out," said her father. "Because this whole thing is absolutely nuts. I can't believe I let myself get suckered into this meeting. I knew what would happen. It always does."

As soon as Katie had stopped crying, her dad made his escape. He didn't even wait until the end of the session.

"See you, kiddo," he'd said to her and given her a quick kiss on the top of her head. He still hadn't looked at her.

After he was gone, Sandy asked her mom to go outside to the waiting room so that he could have a few words with Katie. She was afraid he was going to talk about what had happened, and she would have to come up with excuses for her parents. Instead, he handed her a notebook with a flow-ered cover.

"You may have some emotional reactions to this session," he said. She started to shake her head, but he went on. "If you do, there are two things I want you to do. First, I want you to try to write down what you're feeling. But if you can't, you call me. Normally patients are allowed to call me up until ten o'clock at night. But tonight you can call me anytime you need me. Do that instead of . . . anything that might hurt you. Okay?"

She knew he meant he didn't want her using the scissors. What was scary was that he knew she might. Sometimes it was like he got inside her mind. She wasn't sure she liked it when he did that, but it did make her feel less alone. She looked up at him. He was still holding out the notebook. The easiest way to deal with him would be to take the notebook and tell him what he wanted to hear. She could promise she wouldn't use the scissors and he'd believe her. Adults always believed her. But then she looked at him again. There was something about him. He wasn't shouting or giving orders, but he was very, very serious. She took the notebook.

"I'll try to do what you want," she said slowly. "But I don't know if I can."

"As long as you try," he said. "And thank you for being honest with me."

WHEN SHE got home, she didn't call him.

She didn't write down her feelings.

She did use the scissors.

But that night when she went to sleep, she put the notebook under her pillow.

AT THE END OF the day, Sandy jotted down his observations from the Roskova session. "The family dynamic is a classic for a kid with Katie's disorder," he wrote. "The father abandoned her to the mother at an early age. He suggests that the mother was abusive, which would also be consistent with the disorder. Katie learned there was no one out there for her. So she 'takes care of herself' by cutting to lessen her anxiety.

"In spite of her anger at me, there was a beginning of trust from Katie at the end of the session. But we have a long way to go."

29

The next weeks with Katie marked the kind of slow progress Sandy, after years of practice, had disciplined himself to accept. By temperament he was impatient, but he knew pushing did no good. So he let Katie go at her own pace—which felt like that of molasses pouring on a cold day.

She was still refusing to write in her diary. She still refused to talk about the ways in which she hurt herself or the issues that drove her to do it. She denied strongly that she had ever been mistreated or neglected by either of her parents.

"Since she won't talk about it, I don't know how much she's cutting herself," Sandy said to his wife one night after a particularly frustrating session with Katie. "I have no way of knowing if the disease is escalating. If she's cutting more or deeper. All I do know is, she hasn't had any more episodes like the one in the hallway at her school."

"What about putting her on medication?" his wife asked.

"Not yet. I think I can reach her without that."

He tended to avoid using drugs whenever possible. It wasn't that he had any objection to them, but as long as a patient was reacting to him and the therapy—even if it was only a little bit—he'd rather do without the meds. Katie's case was tricky because she was so clever at faking cooperation.

However, there had been a couple of breakthroughs.

A popular magazine for young women ran an article on

self-mutilation that he xeroxed and gave to Katie. She not only read it, she looked up the book from which the article was taken and went through it too, taking copious notes which they then discussed during her sessions. As long as these conversations remained abstract, she was willing to talk about the subject. But whenever he tried to bring up her own behavior, she shut down on him.

That was true of almost any topic. She was delighted to tell him about the technical aspects of figure skating. Her feelings about her experience as a skater were something else.

"I don't have any feelings about it," she said one day after he'd tried to introduce the subject. "I just try to be the best."

"Isn't that a lot of pressure?"

"Pressure's part of it when you compete." She flashed her big, bright smile.

"That must make it hard to enjoy skating."

Pause. No smile. "Sometimes."

"Do you enjoy it, Katie?"

Long pause. "I don't have to enjoy it," she said in a soft voice.

"But you spend so much time at it. If you're not having a good time . . ."

"That doesn't matter. You don't understand."

"Explain it to me."

"I can't. You always try to make things too simple."

One breakthrough came by accident. He left Katie alone in his office for a few minutes before her session one afternoon to get a drink of water. When he came back he found her studying the family photos on his desk. He wasn't surprised; the pictures, which were informal shots of him with his wife, his two daughters, and their Lhasa Apso, often attracted the attention—and the jealousy—of the kids he treated. Particularly girls like Katie who lacked a strong father figure.

"That's my family," he said. "My daughter Laura was just about your age when it was taken." He prepared himself for questions about his relationship with his girls. Katie threw him a curve.

"That's such a cute little dog," she said. "Do you still have it?"

That's the first time I've been upstaged by a pet, thought Sandy. Should keep me humble.

"Yes, we do. His name is Satchie. He belongs to my daughters, but now that they're both off at college he hangs out with me mostly."

"I've never had a dog or a cat." The tone was so nakedly wistful he almost didn't recognize it as belonging to self-possessed Katie. On an impulse he said, "Sometimes Satchie comes to work with me, especially when I'm seeing clients who don't mind animals."

Her face lit up. "Really?" she breathed.

HE'D TOLD THE truth. He often brought Satchie to work when he and his wife had full schedules. The little guy hated to be left alone all day and he had the office drill down cold. When a patient walked in, he did a fast couple of minutes of meeting and greeting, then he retired to sleep under Sandy's desk. Actually he made a good icebreaker, especially for the very lonely kids.

Of course, there were patients who tried to use him as a distraction to avoid their therapy. When one of those was on the calendar, poor old Satchie had to stay home. But Sandy brought him in for Katie's next session.

Her reaction to the little dog was one of pure delight. She forgot all the reserve of her fifteen years and got down on the floor to play with him. As he watched her, Sandy felt sadly that he was seeing the happy little girl she could have been—but doubted that she ever was.

Finally, it was time to get down to work. "Satchie, come," he called. The Lhasa Apso dutifully trotted over to him. He gave the command to lie down and Satchie went to his spot under the desk.

"Why did you do that?" Katie said in a voice he hadn't

heard before. He turned. She was glaring at him, her hands balled up in angry fists.

"He was having fun," she said. "Why did you stop him?"

"Because you and I have to have a session. Satchie's okay. He knows the rules."

"That's what *you* say. How do you know how he feels?"

Her guard was down—it was an opportunity to make a connection. Thank you, Satchie, he thought as he quickly asked, "Do you know how Satchie feels, Katie?"

She reddened and turned away. "No. Of course I don't."

"But you just got pretty angry at me about something."

"It just seems unfair. He's a dog, so he has to please humans all the time."

"Is there something wrong with that?"

Beat. "I guess not. I was being stupid."

"How do you feel about having to please people, Katie?" he prodded.

"This isn't about me."

"I think it is. You had a very big emotional reaction to the way I was treating Satchie just now. In my experience, when a person responds that strongly to a situation it usually means that something has been triggered inside them."

She seemed to consider what he'd said. For a moment, he thought she was going to address it. Then he saw her pull back.

"I don't have to please anyone," she said.

"Really? It seems to me you have a whole list of folks who have to be happy with you—your teachers at school, your mom, the judges when you skate, your coaches . . ."

"I don't mind . . ."

"Don't you? Not even a little bit?"

Once again she wavered; there was so much pent up inside her that she wanted to say.

But she changed the subject fast. "Look at Satchie," she said, pointing to the dog, who was now snoozing peacefully under the desk. "This dumb conversation is so boring, we've put him to sleep." But for a brief moment she'd let him in.

"We're still going slowly," he wrote in his notes at the end of the session. "But we have made some progress."

Then, suddenly, the way it sometimes happened in therapy, at her next session Katie crashed through to a new plateau.

30

When Katie walked into Sandy's office, she'd been living with a catastrophe for twelve hours. The day before, the unthinkable had happened: Ron had dumped her. "I could continue taking your money, Katherine," he'd said to her mom, "but I'd be cheating you. Katie's a lovely skater, and she's a great girl; I've had a wonderful time working with her, but I just don't think she's championship material."

After he'd delivered his bombshell, Katherine had turned and walked out of the rink. Katie, who was still wearing her skates, hobbled after her.

"Mom, wait for me," she called.

Katherine stopped. Her eyes were sparkling with tears she was trying to blink back. Katie knew she didn't want to cry. "Don't come near me," she said.

"But you have to take me home . . ."

Her mother didn't say anything as she stood fighting for control.

"Please, Mom . . ."

Her mother started walking again.

"Mom, don't leave me . . ." It was Katie who was weeping now.

Katherine whirled on her. "Don't you dare cry. I'm the one who should be crying. I gave up my life for you. My life, do you hear? And for what? For this . . . shit?" She started walking again.

Tears blurring her vision, Katie bent over to unlace her skates; she pulled them off and raced after her mother barefoot. The concrete sidewalk shredded her tights and cut the bottoms of her feet, but she kept on running. She caught up with Katherine in the parking lot. Her mother was sitting in the car, her head cradled in her hands on the steering wheel. Katie got into the car as quietly as she could.

"I'm sorry, Mom," she said.

She knew it was all her fault. And it had nothing to do with her skating. She'd been letting the walls down for Sandy Sherman. That was her sin. She had let him trick her into talking about her secret medicine. He called it self-mutilation, and she'd never actually admitted that she did it, but she'd come close. Too close. She'd almost told him how she felt about skating—that it wasn't fun now because she never won anymore. She'd almost admitted that there were times when she hated it. Even to think that was evil, and she'd come close to saying it out loud. No wonder they'd lost Ron. It was retribution for the thoughts she'd had and the things she'd almost said to Sandy Sherman. She'd betrayed the dream, and now she was being punished. She turned to her mother.

"I'll change, Mom," she said. "You find another coach and I'll change. I'll do it right. Everything'll be okay. You'll see."

And it would be, because she knew what she had to do. She had to stop talking to Sandy Sherman.

SANDY KNEW something was up when Katie walked in the door. She barely said hello. Even the fact that he'd left Satchie at home didn't draw the usual protest. Okay, let's confront this now, he thought.

"Katie, what's wrong?"

"Nothing."

"Come on. You haven't said two words since you got here."

"Sometimes I don't feel like talking."

"That's rough. 'Cause talking's one of the main events in this place."

"Well, maybe I don't want to be here."

"Why not? Have I done something to make you angry?"

"No."

"I think you are mad at me."

"It has nothing to do with you. Why do you always think everything's tied up with you?"

She knew she was making a mistake by talking this much. The game plan had been to freeze him out with her silence. But the words kept pouring out of her mouth. "Things happen to me," she heard herself say, "things happen in other places where it isn't always safe and nice like it is here in this room with you and Satchie."

"Where isn't it safe, Katie?"

She knew she shouldn't answer. She should put back the walls. But the words wouldn't stop.

"People leave you," her voice said. "They walk away and they say they'll come back, but they never do."

Suddenly, horribly, her heart began to pound. She was getting light-headed. No, she prayed, I can't space out. Not here.

"Who left you?" Sandy's voice came at her from very far away. Her heart was bursting now.

"Ron."

"Your coach?" His voice was echoing.

"Yes." Her voice was echoing too. The outline of Sandy's body was starting to get shimmery. His face was blurred. She had to get out of there before it was too late. "Could I go get a drink of water?"

"Are you okay?"

She forced herself to nod. "I'm just thirsty."

"Go ahead."

She took her purse.

Afterward, Sandy told himself he should have seen it coming. But he didn't. He thought she was just trying to give herself a break to regroup. He didn't want to intrude on her. "So you're a therapist, not a mind reader," said his wife when he told her later. But he still felt he should have known.

OF COURSE, he figured it out when she didn't come right back. He rushed into his waiting room, but at first he didn't see her. He opened the door to the hallway and was about to call out her name when he heard a sound like a sigh coming from the corner near the water cooler. He found her on the floor.

At first he thought she might need stitches; she seemed to be bleeding quite a lot. But after he cleaned her up with some antiseptic from his first-aid kit he saw that the cuts were long, not deep.

"You sure did a number on yourself," he said as he swabbed her with hydrogen peroxide. Katie started to sob.

KATIE WAS ANGRY at herself for crying again. She wasn't supposed to do that. But it was a different kind of crying now. She'd lost her fight. The plan to put up the walls and get rid of Sandy Sherman had failed. He was in charge now. And she was crying from relief.

SANDY WAITED until the sobbing stopped. Then he made her sit in a chair and he sat across from her. She'd be relaxed and easy to reach right now, he knew.

"I want you to understand what happened here today," he said. "Because it was a very good thing. I don't mean the fact that you hurt yourself—that's not good, and we're going to work together to stop it.

"What's positive about this is that you did your cutting in my office where you knew I'd find you. You wanted to include me. That means you're ready to start dealing with it now, Katie. Now I think we'll be able to talk about it. And talking—"

"I know," she interrupted. "Talking is your favorite thing in the whole world to do." As weary as she was, she shot him a sly little smile. Serious Katie Roskova was making fun of him. That was real progress.

31

For a while the progress was exciting. Katie started writing in her diary. She read certain sections of it to him after they made an agreement that the rest was private. More important, she was finally willing to talk about the cutting. And the reasons for why she did it. "It began about two years ago," she said hesitantly. "Something had started happening to me . . . it was like there was this thing that would get inside me and take over. I couldn't breathe and my heart would go fast and then . . ." She faltered and looked at him, terrified. "It happens all the time to me now . . . I think I'm crazy . . . My mind just . . . leaves. It goes away." She swallowed hard and added in a terrified whisper, "I call it spacing out."

"What a good name for it," Sandy said calmly.

She looked at him in astonishment. "You know what I'm talking about?"

"Not from firsthand experience, but I've had other patients describe the sensation to me. It sounds like you've come up with a very good way of putting it."

She looked at him with a mixture of relief and disbelief. "I thought it was just me. I thought I was nuts."

"Yes," he said gently, "you've been carrying that big, black fear around for a long time, haven't you?"

She nodded slowly.

"Well, let's throw a little scientific light on the beast, shall we?"

She nodded again—he could almost feel her tension.

"I'm not going to try to tell you that what you do is normal,

Katie, or that everyone does it, because that would be a lie and you'd know it," he said. Then he smiled. "But you're not nuts. Although we could probably say you're on the edge of nuts, if you want to be dramatic about it," he teased. The line won him a nervous little smile. "What you have is classified in the books as a personality disorder. But the good news is, we can fix it," he added. That relaxed her visibly. Good, he thought, now for the rest of the lesson.

"So here's what happens to you when you 'space out.' You experience an emotion that you can't handle—either because it's too strong and painful, or because you've been taught it's something you're not allowed to feel, or some combination of those factors. A typical example of a forbidden emotion would be anger." Katie was watching him intently. He couldn't tell if he was getting through. "Since your mind can't handle the feeling, you have what is, in essence, an extremely strong anxiety attack," he went on. "That's why you have trouble catching your breath and your heart begins to race. But you don't stop at that. Because the response that is triggered is too powerful for you, you enter what we call a dissociated state. Which is a fancy way of saying your mind goes blank until the threatening feeling dissipates. It's as if you'd fainted but you're still conscious."

"It's so scary when it happens," Katie whispered.

"Of course it is, and that's why you've figured out a way to stop it. At some point you learned that if you inflict pain on yourself, it focuses your mind and keeps it from dissociating. You give yourself a physical pain to concentrate on instead of the mental pain you can't accept."

Katie flashed him a little grin that was half wry, half fearful. "And that's not totally insane?" she asked softly.

"Technically speaking, you're in a psychotic state when you do it, so as I said, you can't call it normal behavior. But to me there's something beautiful about the way the human mind works out a problem like this. It took creativity and resourcefulness to come up with a solution like this. And once we teach you how to handle your feelings in a more positive way, you can liberate that creative, resourceful mind of yours for other things. Then I figure the sky's the limit for you." She smiled happily. He had a sense of the burden that had been lifted off her. Nothing like a little knowledge to scare away the monsters, he thought.

IN HER NEXT session, she volunteered to tell him about the first time she'd cut herself.

"I'd been spacing out for five or six months and it scared me," she began. "One day I fell when I was skating and I cut open my knee." She paused and wrinkled up her nose. "I hate talking about this," she said.

"It's okay. I have a good idea of what's coming."

"I was starting to space out—dissociate—when I fell. And it was just like you said—I found out if I thought about how my knee felt, the spacey feeling stopped.

"The next time I spaced out, I was at home. So I picked up one of my skates and used the toe of it on my leg. Right here." She pointed to her inner thigh. "But that made a big scrape; there was too much blood. And it wasn't a good place because you could see the mark through my tights. So now I use a scissors, and I do it on my arm." She gave him a little smile that said "problem solved."

There were other things she still was not willing to talk about. School and friends rated no more than a contemptuous shrug. And her parents were completely off-limits. Sandy had gotten the idea from Peter Roskova's remarks that Katie's mother might have been physically abusive during the time when she was Katie's skating teacher. He asked Katie about it.

"My mom was strict because she had to be," she said primly. "If Mozart's father hadn't made him practice, we wouldn't have all the great works he left behind."

And why do I have the feeling you memorized that little tidbit at your mother's knee? Sandy thought. He wondered if Ms. Roskova had ever thought about the fact that Mozart's life was quite miserable and ended when he was thirty-five.

"So it sounds as if you have no problems with your mother, Katie," he said.

"We have a few disagreements, but they're not important. I'm very lucky." And there was no way to get her to say more about Katherine.

Discussions of her father were also dismissed.

"Do you think there's a parallel in your mind between Ron stopping his work with you and your dad leaving?" he asked.

"You mean, did Ron 'trigger' something?"

"Exactly."

"No way," she said. "Sorry to disappoint you."

She hated the idea that one incident or feeling could bring back others. He knew it made her feel out of control.

"I'll have to watch out for you," she told Satchie at the end of her session that day. "You might trigger me into thinking I'm a dog."

"Katie still will not confront the core issues that bother her," Sandy wrote in his notes.

However, she was very willing to make fun of him. Well, you win some and you lose some.

"I NEED TO DO something to push her just enough to make her take some risks," he said to his wife. "The problem is, if I shake her too much, she could stop trusting me."

There were different approaches he could take with her at this point. He was still mulling them over when he got a phone call that helped him make up his mind.

It came at the end of the day as he was about to leave the office. He thought about not answering, but years of training kicked in. He picked up the phone. "Dr. Sherman, my name is Jenny Moran," said a clear, eager voice. "I'm Katie Roskova's English teacher, and I'd like to speak to you about her. I hope that's all right. Ilene Santiago seemed to feel that it would be inappropriate for any of us here at the school to interfere with your work."

Not for the first time he wondered where Ilene Santiago got her ideas. "I figure we're all in this together when it comes to these kids," he said. "What's up with Katie?"

"I'm worried about her. Ever since she had that episode in the hallway she's been shutting everyone out. Naturally I understand why she's doing it; teenagers can be very cruel, particularly to a kid like Katie, who's already a bit of an outsider. But now she's totally isolated. She skips lunch. I never see her walking with anyone in the halls; she's even stopped answering questions in class. I don't know how much of this she's told you. My sense of her is, she'd cover up—even with a therapist."

"I'm afraid you're right; Katie hasn't let me know how bad things are for her in school. And she doesn't need the kind of isolation you're describing."

The teacher sighed. "I had hoped she'd cut back on that brutal schedule of hers, but she's still racing out of here early and coming in late so she can work with her skating coach," she said.

So Katie and her mom had decided not to tell the school about losing Ron. Or was Katie maintaining the fiction by herself out of pride? Either way, it wasn't good, nor was the friendless existence Katie was living. He thanked Jenny and said good-bye. His mind was made up.

THAT NIGHT HE said to his wife, "I may be pushing her before she's ready, but I want to start Katie in a group."

32

Katie hated the whole idea of group therapy. When Sandy suggested it, she hoped her mom would refuse. But Katherine, who seemed to have gotten over her anger, had been too focused on finding a new skating coach to care.

"It's not as though you have anything better to do," she said when Katie mentioned this new plan. "We'll go along with it. No need to make waves right now." Katie had a feeling her mom was up to something. But whatever it was, it wouldn't keep Katie out of group therapy.

Sandy tried to prepare her for it. "It may bring up some competitive feelings for you at first," he said. "You'll be sharing my attention with five other girls and you're used to one-on-one. But you'll also be sharing with them. And that'll be worth it."

But Katie wasn't sure it was going to be worth it when she walked into his office before her first group session. In fact, she thought it was going to be awful. What if these new girls didn't like her? What if they thought she was weird, or nuts? They'd never find out about what she did—the cutting—because she would never tell them. She was absolutely determined about that.

But why had Sandy done this to her? She wanted to demand an explanation. He was supposed to protect her. He was always going on and on about how much he wanted her to trust him. Well, after this she would never trust him again as long as she lived.

"You're a little early," Sandy said as he led her into the office.

Actually she was very early. She wanted to get the jump on the enemy. If she was there first, hopefully she could meet the other girls one at a time as they came in. She didn't want to walk into a group. She looked around the office. The furniture had been rearranged so it formed a circle with his desk at the head of it. It hadn't occurred to her before that moment that she would have to pick a place to sit. In her private therapy sessions she always had her own spot on the couch. But was it only hers? It suddenly occurred to her that this office was used by lots of patients. For all she knew, several of them thought of her spot on the couch as their own. Suddenly, claiming her own territory for this session seemed very important.

She considered the possibilities. If she sat across from Sandy's desk she'd have more of his attention, but she'd lose her place on the couch. If she sat in the corner where it was dark, she could hide better but she'd be out of Sandy's direct sight line.

She was still debating when the buzzer went off.

"It's Beth," said the voice on the intercom. Quickly, Katie settled herself on the couch. The other girls were coming in.

33

There were five girls in the group: Beth, Elsie, Isabella ("Call me Izzy"), Pam, and Jodi. And now Katie Roskova. Maybe. Katie told herself the jury was still out on that.

Beth took it upon herself to introduce Katie to everyone as they came in. It was easy to see why Beth needed help, Katie thought. She was fat. She wasn't slightly chubby, or a little heavy, or any of the nice ways people tried to say it. She was fat. After a lifetime of controlling her own weight, Katie had a prejudice against fat people. This made her feel a little guilty, but she couldn't help it. Not that Beth seemed to care that she was such a complete slob. "This is Pam," she said, indicating a tall, painfully thin girl who was hugging her coat to herself. The girl's hair was thin and brittle-looking, and her eyes seemed huge. Because her face was so gaunt it was impossible to tell how old she was. "Pammie and I are the eating disorder girls," said Beth. "Guess which one of us is the anorexic." Pam said hi and sat down quickly.

"Izzy's here because of her lousy fashion sense," Beth continued. "She really thinks all those studs she's got are attractive." Izzy gave her the finger. Katie decided she was probably fifteen or sixteen; her brown hair was uncombed, her jeans had the obligatory tear across the left knee. Small silver rings adorned holes in her ears that ran all the way up the sides, there was a stud in her nose, and two mean-looking pins were pierced through the flesh of her right eyebrow.

"Show Katie what else you've got," Beth commanded. Remarkably, Izzy lifted her T-shirt to display not only the pierced navel Katie had expected, but also an elaborate tattoo of a snake curled around it. When she breathed, it seemed to move. "Gross, isn't it?" said Beth.

"Next week I'm getting a spike in my tongue just for you," said Izzy.

"Elsie flips out and cuts herself." Beth indicated a pale, well-dressed girl with red-rimmed eyes who looked as if she'd been crying recently. Katie was sure she was older than the rest of them.

"And Jodi's here because she's failing all her classes and her mommy thinks she's getting in with a very bad crowd at school," said Beth, finishing her round of introductions.

"Screw my mommy," said Jodi, who wore a T-shirt that said "Nuke Gay Whales for Jesus" and skin-hugging tights. "She's the one with the problem."

"And then there's Beth, who eats everything that isn't nailed down," said Izzy.

"Hey, I have to keep up my strength, I have responsibilities," said Beth in a way that was meant to be light, but Katie thought she noticed anger under it.

Sandy seemed to notice it too, because he stepped in quickly and said, "Okay, Beth, thank you for doing the honors." Beth executed a little half bow from her seat, which got her a small laugh.

"Welcome to the zoo, Katie," said Izzy. "So what's your disease?" It was the last thing Katie expected. For a moment she thought she was going to pass out.

"I don't . . . I mean, I'm not . . ." she stammered.

"You're not a sicko like the rest of us? Come on. Why are you here?"

"Lay off her, Izzy." The words came from the skeleton girl, Pam. She smiled at Katie and her face looked like a Halloween mask. What am I doing here with these people? Katie thought wildly. She tried frantically to make eye contact with Sandy. I will never forgive you for this, her look told him. He seemed to get the message.

"Pam does have a point," he said. "Maybe we should give Katie a little time to adjust before we ask her to participate."

Izzy sulked. "Everything I do is wrong," she said.

"I'm just trying to keep this a comfortable place for everyone," said Sandy calmly. "That wasn't a criticism."

"It sure sounded like one," said Izzy.

"And how does that make you feel?" asked Sandy the way he always did in Katie's private sessions.

It was as if everyone had been waiting for that question, or one like it. They leaned forward, prodding and cajoling Izzy until she admitted that it wasn't really Sandy she was mad at but her father. That seemed to open the floodgates. Everyone had an incident to relate or a comment to offer. Sometimes they were kind with each other, sometimes they were harsh. Jodi and Izzy were particularly tough about telling the others to cut the bull.

At first Katie sat back, grateful that she was no longer in the hot seat, and tuned them all out. But then, gradually, she started paying attention. The conversation—if you could call it that—was a bit of a free-for-all. But there was also a weird kind of logic to it too. Sandy was keeping them on track; and because everyone was working on being honest, more and more of their stories came out.

Beth, Katie gathered, was the oldest of four. Her mother was divorced and worked at two jobs to support the family. The fat girl seemed to have full responsibility for her younger siblings. She referred to them as "the kids," and it sounded as if she spent her life taking care of them—and eating.

"I blew my diet again last night," she reported with tears in her eyes. "My mom worked late and I had to feed the kids again and it made me so mad, I just blew it . . ."

IT TURNED OUT that Izzy wasn't in therapy just because of the disgusting things she did to her body. Her mother and her stepfather also hated her boyfriend, who was ten years older than she was and did sound kind of terrible to Katie. Izzy had run away from home three times to be with him, and she was convinced that someday she and Mel were going to go off into the sunset together.

"Fat chance," said Pam.

"Look who's talking," cracked Beth.

PAM SEEMED TO be willing to talk about everyone else's problems. But whenever anyone, including Sandy, tried to direct the session toward her, she clammed up. Katie gathered that her dad was a very successful lawyer. Her mom she dismissed tersely as "that wimp."

JODI'S MOM AND dad were getting a divorce because Jodi's mom had a new boyfriend. Jodi wanted to live with her father but he'd already moved out of state and she didn't want to leave her school, her younger brother, or her boyfriend. Her mom, who worked for a PR firm in New York, would be staying in the area and wanted custody of both of her kids, but Jodi was furious at her and called her "the Slut."

"Thanks to the Slut my life is over," she said angrily. Then she started to cry. Pam handed her a box of tissues. Izzy, who was sitting next to her on the couch, hugged her. Then Beth started crying too, which for some reason made them all laugh.

Katie sat, silently watching the four girls laughing together and felt left out—and jealous. Which was really weird, because she'd always been the outsider in her school and it hadn't bothered her—not too much anyway.

But she didn't expect to feel like an outsider in Sandy Sherman's office. He'd set it up as a safe place, where she belonged. She turned to him. He was focused on Jodi, who was ranting and raving about her mom's new boyfriend. She wanted to get Sandy's attention. It was up to him to smooth the way for her with these girls. He was running the group; he could make them include her.

AS HE SHEPHERDED his group through the session, Sandy kept his antennae out for signs that Katie was in trouble. In the beginning she'd seemed a little overwhelmed by her first group experience—which was a natural reaction. But as the hour passed he could see her wanting to get involved. Now she was looking to him to help her break in. Which he could do by simply directing a question at her.

Not just yet, Katie, he thought to himself. Let's see if you can handle this on your own, without me.

KATIE WAS GETTING sick of being invisible. But the others seemed to be such a tight group. "They don't need you, stupid," said the voice in her head.

Suddenly there was a silence in the marathon talk. Now's my chance, Katie thought. But before she could think of something to say, Pam turned to Elsie, who had been quietly hunched in her chair.

"You haven't said a word, Elsie," she said gently. "What's going on?"

Katie sat forward. She'd been wondering about the silent Elsie who "flipped out and cut herself." Now she wanted to see how the others dealt with her.

"There's nothing to say . . ." Elsie began.

"Shit," said Izzy.

"Izzy, knock it off," said Beth. "Talk, Elsie."

"Last night I . . ." Elsie stopped and struggled not to cry.

"Hang on," said Beth. She picked up the box of tissues and elaborately handed it to Elsie. "Okay, hit it," she said as everyone laughed and Elsie gave her a grateful half smile. She closed her eyes.

"Last night I did it again," she said. "I took a razor blade out of my mom's drawer in the bathroom and I cut myself."

"Oh, Elsie," mourned Beth, "you were doing so well."

"I haven't done it in five weeks and two days," said Elsie.

"But who's counting?" Jodi added, which got another laugh. The group seemed to realize that Elsie needed them to keep it light for her.

"It was the longest I've ever gone," said Elsie.

Katie sat very still as she took in this horrible news. Was it really possible that you could stop the behavior for such a long period of time and then still have to hurt yourself again?

"Why did you do it?" she asked. "Did something"—she paused over the hated word—"trigger it?"

Elsie shook her head.

"But something must have," Katie persisted. "I mean . . . I thought once you stopped doing it, you stopped."

Elsie gave her a quick, knowing glance. "You do it too, don't you?" she said.

The room became very quiet. Sandy realized he was holding his breath.

Katie looked around at the five girls who were staring at her. They were waiting. She'd never told anyone but Sandy what she did. She'd never told anyone her own age anything important. She took a deep breath.

"Yes, I do it too," she said quietly.

Congratulations, Katie, Sandy thought.

WHEN HER MOM came to pick her up after group therapy, Katie was making awkward conversation with Izzy, Beth, and Jodi, who were also waiting for their rides.

"How old are you?" Beth asked her. Katie knew she'd offered the question as an icebreaker and was grateful.

"I'll be sixteen next month. On the twentieth."

"I used to think life would be so great when I was sixteen," said Jodi as she dragged on her cigarette. Both Jodi and Izzy lit up the second they were outdoors. "Two weeks after my sixteenth birthday the Slut dropped her bomb and life's been shit ever since."

Katie felt she should say something but couldn't figure out what. Fortunately, before she had to, Katherine pulled up and honked the horn.

"See you next week," she said to the girls and she ran to her mother's car.

When she got in, Katherine was frowning. Katie figured her mom had seen the cigarettes.

"Who are those girls?" Katherine demanded.

"They're in my group," said Katie.

"They look like a bunch of delinquents."

Katie shrugged and waited for the tirade against group therapy that had to be coming. Katherine surprised her.

"Well, there's nothing we can do about it yet," she said. "We'll just have to put up with it for a while longer." But she smiled to herself as if she had a secret that pleased her a lot. She was definitely up to something.

"What did you think of the group session?" Sandy asked at their next meeting.

"It was okay," said Katie.

Even though the group scared her, she was looking forward to the next one more than she wanted him to know. She liked the seriousness of the other girls. And the fact that they were committed to telling the truth. It made the group feel like a safe place to be. Even though there were times when the conversations got brutally honest.

"Katie, do you ever just let your mom have it?" Izzy asked her one day. Katie had just told the group about the way her mother had blamed her when they'd lost Ron as her coach.

"No. I don't like to fight with her," said Katie.

"Because she's so damned wonderful?" Jodi scoffed.

"She does what she has to. It's for my own good," said Katie.

"Jesus. Get a life, Katie," Izzy said in disgust.

But what was nice about it was, she really did want Katie to get a life. Because somehow if Katie got a life, then it meant maybe Izzy could solve her problems too. There was a connection between them all that was more intense than any she'd ever felt with anyone except her mom. And they didn't want anything from her.

"Katie's still having trouble confronting her anger," Sandy wrote in his notes. "But she seems to be forming some nice, strong bonds with the girls in the group. Unfortunately, according to her English teacher, she still hasn't come out of her shell at school. She remains far too isolated when she's there."

SCHOOL WAS THE place where Katie's loneliness hurt so much it was almost like a physical pain. She still hadn't returned to eating in the cafeteria; as the weather got warmer, she got into the habit of taking an apple and some yogurt to the parking lot and reading during lunchtime. She soon discovered she wasn't the only one who hung out there.

"Hey," Dave Malloy called from across the lot. He was leaning against his new red BMW. It was his second. He'd already totaled a similar one his dad had given him six months earlier. On either side of him were his two pals. Josh was holding a brown paper bag with a bottle in it. As Katie turned and started toward them, he quickly thrust it into the front seat of the car.

"Want to go for a ride?" Dave asked.

"Now?" asked Katie. Her mouth was suddenly dry. Her legs were threatening to stop holding her up.

"Sure," he said.

"You can't leave school grounds in the middle of the day," Katie said. Dave scowled, but his two friends burst into high-pitched laughter.

"I can do whatever the hell I want," said Dave angrily. "And I don't need some crazy little bitch telling me different."

"I didn't mean . . ." Katie started, but then stopped because he'd gotten into his car. "You coming?" he demanded of his friends. They scrambled in just in time. Dave turned on the ignition and peeled out.

Katie watched him go. This was the second time he'd hurt her feelings and made her feel stupid. But he had asked her to go for a drive. Her legs were still wobbly.

JENNY MORAN'S classroom overlooked the parking lot. She'd decided to stay in during her lunch hour to grade papers, and she happened to glance up and see Katie talking to Dave Malloy and his friends. As she watched the four-some, she had to resist an urge to run out and drag Katie away.

Dave was one of the few kids in the school Jenny found almost impossible to like. His pals were relatively harm-less—mere acolytes trying to keep up with him. But Dave was a mean-spirited bully—in Jenny's opinion—who had been getting away with murder all of his young life thanks to his own talent as an athlete and Mr. Malloy's money. Whenever the football coach couldn't bail Dave out, his rich, indulgent, largely absentee father did. As far as Jenny was concerned, he was the worst possible candidate for a friendship—or anything else—with vulnerable little Katie Roskova.

Jenny waited until the lunch hour was almost over. Then she went out into the hallway to wait.

KATIE HAD TO pass Ms. Moran's room to get to her biology class. She wasn't expecting the English teacher to ambush her on the way.

"I'd like to see you in my room for a minute," said Ms. Moran in a way that made it clear she wasn't going to take no for an answer. Katie followed her into the classroom.

"I know you've been having a difficult time in school lately," said Ms. Moran. Katie gave her the blank stare she'd picked up from Izzy. It was very cool, and she'd been dying to use it on somebody.

"I saw you with Dave Malloy just now," Ms. Moran went on. "Dave's got a lot of problems, Katie. I do hope you know that."

This time Katie gave her the blank stare for real. "He's not a friend of mine," she said.

"I'm glad to hear it." Ms. Moran hesitated for a second, then said, "Katie, if you ever need to talk, I'm available."

Katie nodded politely and quickly left the room.

"WHAT IS SHE doing, hanging around with a kid like Dave Malloy?" Jenny demanded of Ilene later that afternoon.

"Katie's a girl whose self-esteem is so low she'd rather hurt herself than express needs and feelings that might offend others. That's not the profile of a girl who makes healthy choices in relationships," said Ilene. "And it can get worse as she gets older. She's lucky she's getting help now."

Oh, yes, Jenny thought, Katie's so lucky.

35

"My dad didn't show up again last week," said Beth. "I don't mind for myself, but it was hard on my sister Francie. She's only eight and she doesn't understand."

"And you do?" said Izzy.

"I got over needing my dad a long time ago."

"Bull," said Jodi. "You still get pissed if he doesn't show."

"I bet you ate a whole quart of ice cream after he did that," said Izzy.

"No," Beth began, but suddenly Katie couldn't stand it anymore.

"What's the big deal?" she heard herself demand. "So what if her father doesn't visit?"

"She's trying to say it doesn't bother her," said Elsie.

"So maybe it doesn't. Maybe she doesn't care. Maybe she knows what she's talking about and the rest of you should just shut up."

Izzy and Jodi exchanged a glance. Before either of them could say anything, Sandy jumped in. "What's going on, Katie?" he asked. "Why does this upset you so much?"

"I'm not upset. I just think Beth—"

"Talk about you, Katie. What about you?"

"I don't think Beth misses her father."

"What about your father?"

"I never see him. So what?" Suddenly she was aware that they were all looking at her. Even Sandy was sitting back, waiting. "My dad is too busy," she said very calmly. "He has a new girlfriend and she takes up a lot of his time. And besides, when he's with my mom, all they do is fight. I'd rather he didn't come around."

"Do you fight with him? When your mom's not there?" asked Pam gently.

"I don't see him much . . . I haven't in a while . . . We're not close."

"What does that mean, Katie?" asked Sandy. "Not being close to your dad?"

"He's not there."

"Why isn't he, Katie?"

"He left us . . ." Tears were starting in her eyes. She couldn't control her voice.

"Why did he leave?"

"He didn't care . . ." Pam brought her the tissue box and placed it in front of her.

"What didn't he care about, Katie?" asked Sandy.

"He never cared what happened to me," Katie sobbed.

"I miss my dad too," Jodi whispered. She put her arm around Katie and started to cry.

From across the room there was an explosion. "What about me?" yelled Beth. "We were talking about me and Katie took over." She was glaring at Sandy. "She can't do that."

"Why don't you tell Katie?" said Sandy. Katie felt herself start to tremble as Beth turned to her. "You never talk about anything in group unless somebody else brings it up first," she said. "Then you hog all the attention for yourself and I'm sick of it."

Katie wanted to sink through the floor and disappear forever.

"Sounds to me like you and Katie have a lot in common," said Sandy. "She can't talk about her emotions so she talks about yours. And you can't talk about yours, so you talk about your sister Francie's. Why don't you tell Katie how you feel about your father, Beth?"

Beth leaned forward and locked eyes with Katie.

"I hate his guts," said Beth. "And I wish he'd come back."

Then she started to cry. Katie got up and walked across the room to her. She knelt down and took the large girl in her arms.

"BREAKTHROUGH!" Sandy wrote in his notes. "Katie is starting to confront her feelings about her parents in group."

36

"I don't want to talk about your father," said Katherine. "Stop asking me all these questions."

"I just want to know why you married him. Did you ever love him?"

"I married him because I was stupid."

"But—"

"Katie, leave me alone."

"I want to talk about it."

"Well, I don't. This is what you're learning in that damn therapy of yours, isn't it?"

"He's my father, I have a right to know about him."

"I suppose that's what your therapist tells you. Well, you can tell him from me that it's none of his damn business."

"He's never said anything like that . . ."

"Don't you talk back to me."

"I'm not . . ."

"If you ever do it again, I'll get on the phone with your precious Sandy Sherman and tell him what I think of him. Do you hear me?"

"Mom, I'm the one who wanted . . ."

"You want to know about your father? I'll tell you about him. He's a selfish, spoiled son of a bitch."

"WHY IS SATCHIE in that cage?" Katie demanded. She'd walked into Sandy's office for her private session, and stopped abruptly when she'd seen the little dog in his carrier.

"Satchie's been having a bad day," Sandy said. "Sometimes he gets a little restless and—"

"Take him out of there," she said, interrupting him. "Right now. Take him out." She turned large, pain-filled eyes to him. "Please," she begged.

Sandy opened the door of the carrier. Satchie, who was no fool, ran to his benefactress, who scooped him up in her arms.

"What does it mean to be in a cage, Katie?" Sandy asked softly. She buried her face in the dog's silky fur. "Katie?" he asked again.

She looked out the windows at the trees for a long time. "It means being punished," she said finally.

"What's the worst punishment you can imagine?"

She turned to look at him. Her eyes were dark with sadness now, and she was holding Satchie very close.

"Being alone," she said. Then she added so softly he almost couldn't hear her, "Losing Mama."

"And if you lost Mama, then what?"

"I don't know . . . I don't know if I could live without Mama." It wasn't teenage hyperbole. She meant it.

Sometimes you had to let your patients sit with their private demons. Sometimes you had to try a little exorcism. Knowing when to do what was a judgment call that never got any easier to make.

"Katie, we all want to love certain people in our lives. And we should, it's natural and normal. But sometimes the people we love make demands that aren't good for us. Then we have to learn to separate from that person—or at least from the part of the person that makes the inappropriate demands. You have the right to take care of yourself, Katie.

"Above all, you shouldn't have to be afraid that you'll lose the person you love if you do the wrong thing. That's like living your life with a gun to your head. And pleasing the other person should never keep you from doing what you have to do for yourself. That's not good for anyone. Including the person you care about so much."

She didn't look up at him again, so he had no way of knowing if she'd gotten what he was trying to say.

37

"Okay, who wants to start?" Sandy asked the group.

"I do," Katie heard herself say.

Beth pretended to fall off her chair and everyone laughed.

"What do you want to talk about, Katie?" Sandy asked.

Suddenly she was afraid she couldn't do it. For two days she'd been planning what she wanted to say. But now . . .

"I . . . I had a fight with my mom," she blurted out. It wasn't what she'd rehearsed. She started to backtrack quickly. "My mom's okay," she said. "I mean, most of the time we get along and—"

"And yada, yada, yada," Jodi broke in. "What did you fight about?"

"It's not important."

"Tell us, and we'll decide that," said Izzy.

"What happened?" asked Elsie. She was leaning forward and looking very intense. There were times when Elsie scared Katie. She tried to tell herself it wasn't because Elsie did the same thing she did. Elsie called herself "a cutter." Sometimes she called Katie one too.

"What do you mean?" Katie parried.

"When you and your mom fought, what happened?"

"She yelled."

"That's all?"

"She called me a name—sort of. I don't think I want to talk about this anymore."

"Why not, Katie?" asked Sandy.

"Because my mom isn't here to defend herself."

"The Slut isn't here either, but that doesn't stop me," said Jodi.

"Why does your mother need to defend herself, Katie?" asked Sandy.

"Because I'm talking about her behind her back, and it isn't fair."

"Why?" he prodded. "What are you going to say about her?"

"Nothing. There's nothing to say."

"Sometimes when my dad had been drinking he'd come home and he'd beat the shit out of me," said Elsie.

"Well, my mom's not like that. She'd never . . ." Katie stopped short. Memories came flooding back. Things she hadn't thought about for years. Things she never let herself think about. Because the walls would really fall down if she did. And she would space out and never come back. She looked around. The faces of the other girls were starting to get blurry. The room was starting to shimmer. Soon her heart would start to pound and she wouldn't be able to breathe.

"What is it, Katie?" Sandy moved to her quickly. He was in front of her now. It was hard to see his face except for his eyes, but she could tell he was concerned. "Are you all right?" he asked. "Do you need to stop?"

Katie tried to nod. She wasn't sure if she actually did or not.

"Katie," Sandy said sharply, "Katie, look at me. You're going to be all right. Do you hear me?" His voice was firm and strong. It pulled her back. "Just look at me. You're not going anywhere." She made herself focus on his eyes. The room stopped shimmering. Gradually his face became clear again. He smiled. "Good girl," he said.

"What the hell was that all about?" demanded Izzy.

"No big deal," said Sandy as he went back to his desk. "It's just that sometimes we have to back off until we're ready to handle certain things. Everyone in this room knows about that. Now, who's next?"

— ❈ —

THE SESSION WENT on as if she wasn't there. It was like being disqualified for a competition. She'd gotten herself all revved up for a battle, and now she had to sit on the sidelines while the rest of them were still out there fighting. They were talking and laughing and crying. She was silent. Again. She always had to be silent. It was so frustrating. Of course, she was grateful to Sandy for bailing her out when she was in trouble earlier. But now . . .

"When I was little, my mom was my first skating teacher," she said loudly. She knew she was interrupting someone, but she didn't care. She wasn't even sure who it was. Everyone turned to look at her. She had the floor.

"When she was teaching me, I wasn't always . . . I didn't always pay attention," she continued in the same loud voice. "I was very little. So sometimes my mom would pull my hair—to make me work harder. She said she had to be strict. Or she would pinch my arm. I always used to have bruises on it. I have scars on my arms now. But they're farther down, near the wrist.

"One time she yanked my arm so hard the doctor thought my shoulder was dislocated. But it was only wrenched."

Should I let this go on? Sandy wondered. Katie seemed okay, but she'd nearly lost it before. He looked at the other girls. They were so intent on Katie, they were almost breathing with her. They knew how difficult this was and they were willing her to get through it. She won't find a safer place anywhere to get this out, he decided.

"I never told anyone my mom was the one who hurt me," Katie went on. "Because I thought it was all my fault. She was my mother. She said I deserved it. I believed her."

Tears were running down Elsie's cheeks, Sandy noticed. No one else seemed to. All attention was on Katie. It was as if they were watching someone walk across a high wire without a net. Well, he thought, in a way, they were.

"My mom never spanked me," Katie said. "But sometimes I made her so mad when I didn't do things right that she couldn't keep from hurting me. And I was very expensive, because I kept growing out of my costumes and my skates.

My dad complained all the time about the money I cost. So I understood why she lost her temper . . ."

She paused. She seemed to be struggling for control. Sandy felt himself tense.

"But then one day when I was about six years old, she . . ." She stopped, then started again. "One day my mother . . ." She threw an agonized look at Sandy.

"That's enough for now, Katie," he said gently. "You did beautifully. Be proud of yourself." She nodded and leaned back in her chair, exhausted. The room was quiet. Finally, Izzy spoke.

"Don't you ever just want to hurt your mother?" she asked quietly.

"Whatever your mother did to you, you didn't deserve it, Katie," Beth said.

38

Katie and her mother drove home in silence after the group. Katie couldn't remember ever feeling so tired.

"You're awfully quiet," said Katherine when they were in the house. "Must have been big doings in that group of yours today."

"Not really," said Katie.

"Something must have happened. Usually when you get out of there you're jabbering away and I can't shut you up."

Her mom probably didn't even mean it to be insulting. She'd certainly said worse before. But something inside Katie wasn't going to let it go. "Don't you ever just want to hurt her?" Izzy had asked.

"Mom, do you remember when you broke my ribs?" Katie asked in a hard, steely voice that she herself didn't recognize. Her mother whirled around to face her. "What are you talking about?" she demanded.

"When I was six," the new steely-voiced Katie went on. "I was learning to do a jump—it was a toe loop—and I fell and I didn't want to get up, and you said I had to. And then when I said my ankle hurt, you got so mad you pulled me up off the ice and you threw me against the barricade of the rink. And you broke my ribs."

"No," her mother said in a voice that was so soft it was almost a whisper.

"It happened, Mom. Remember when I lied to the doctor for you? I said I fell while I was practicing."

"No."

"Yes. You stopped teaching me right after that."

"It wasn't that way!" Her mother's voice was getting louder now, and shrill. "I had to be strict with you. You were so lazy."

"So you broke my ribs. Dad knew about it. You had a big fight. I bet if I called him up, he'd remember."

Katherine started toward her, her face full of fury. "I won't have this, Katie," she warned. "You better stop. I won't have a smart-mouth kid."

"What are you going to do, hit me?"

Her mom lifted her hand. For a moment Katie thought she was going to follow through and hit. But Katherine backed off.

"I know who's behind this," she said. "This comes from that goddamn therapist. And those little screw-ups in your group. They put you up to this. They tell you to talk this way to your own mother."

"No. They just tell me to remember what happened. Like the time you threw me into the barricade."

"You told them about that?"

"Yes," Katie lied.

The look on Katherine's face changed abruptly from one of rage to one of bewilderment and pain. "You talked to them about me?" she asked softly. "You talked to strangers about me behind my back?"

For the first time, Katie felt a little unsure of herself.

"I tell them about me, and sometimes you're a part of it," she said.

Katherine was shaking her head in disbelief. "You're my daughter. How could you humiliate me like that?"

"I didn't. I just told them what I was feeling—"

"You stuck a knife in my back."

"Mom, it's not like that in group. Nobody's judging anyone. We're just talking about what's bothering us."

"And that's me."

"Not just you. Mom, I have problems . . ."

"And I caused them. So now you have to go to strangers to

help you get rid of the terrible problems your mother the monster gave you. I understand." She turned and walked away.

"Mom, please listen to me . . ."

"I don't want to talk anymore."

"You're not a monster . . ."

Katherine turned back. Her eyes were glistening with tears. "I'm not? Then why does my only daughter hate me?"

"I don't. Look, Mom, I never should have started this—"

"You're all I have, Katie." The tears were rolling down her mother's cheeks now. "You're all I've ever had. When you were born, when they brought you in to me, I looked at you and I thought, For the first time I have someone who will love me. Finally, there's someone in my life who won't turn on me."

"Mom, I'm sorry. I picked a fight with you and I shouldn't have—"

"I know I'm a hard person, Katie. I've had to be. My life hasn't been easy."

"I know, Mom."

Katherine was crying now—with sobs that seemed to be coming from somewhere deep inside her. She sat at the kitchen table and buried her head in her hands and wept. Katie moved to her and reached out to stroke her hair. Katherine grabbed her hand and turned to look up at her with a red, tear-stained face. "I had to give you discipline, even if you hated me for it. I had to make you tough so you could win. Everything I've done, I did for you, Katie. So you could have it all."

"I know that, Mom. Please don't cry."

"Do you remember when you won your first competition? You were a little tiny thing—the smallest child on the ice. People used to gasp when they saw you skate. I knew then you had it. I knew you could be a star."

It had been so long since Katherine had told her she was going to be a star. When she was little, it had been her bedtime story every night before she went to sleep.

"I can still do it, Mom," she whispered. "I can."

"No," said her mother sadly. "You don't want our dream anymore. Now you want to be like everybody else. You want to be ordinary."

"No . . ."

"Yes. You're angry with me because I wanted the best for you and I pushed you. I don't want you to skate if you're going to be angry with me. I can't take that, Katie."

"I'm not angry, Mama." Her mom was still holding her hand. Katie stroked it.

"I love you, Katie," said Katherine softly. "No matter what, I've always loved you."

"I know, Mama. I'm sorry I made you cry."

And I'll never do it again, she thought. I won't let you down. And I'll make the dream come true.

"You're sure you want to do this?" Sandy asked.

Katie couldn't look at him. If he saw her face, he'd know what she really felt.

"Yes, I want to quit the group."

"But why? You were doing so well."

Because things happen in group that I can't control. Things that make me so angry that I fight with my mother. And that can't happen. I have to quit because it's too dangerous for me.

That was what she wanted to tell him. What she said was, "I don't like it. It's not for me."

"Look, Katie, I know a lot of things surfaced for you in the last session. Sometimes when that happens a patient will want to pull back. They may even regress for a while. It's all part of the process. Why don't you stick with the group for now and we'll talk about this again in a couple of weeks . . ."

If she went back again to the group, she wouldn't be able to leave it. And she couldn't do that to her mom. Katherine had been so happy when Katie made her decision.

"One down, one to go," she'd said gleefully. "Too bad we can't get rid of your damn shrink too."

When she said it, Katie had a moment of panic. She didn't want to stop therapy. Sandy's office was the one place where she could be herself. She was accepted there—more important, she mattered. Fortunately, the school wouldn't let her stop seeing Sandy, so she still had her lifeline. But the group was different—that was optional.

"Are you saying I have to go to the group?" she demanded. She crossed her arms across her chest and scowled at him the way Jodi scowled when she talked about the Slut.

"You know that's not the way it works. I can't force you to do something you don't want to do. I wouldn't try."

"Well, I don't want any more group therapy."

Suddenly he was tired—and so damn angry. It was the waste of it—the sheer, stupid waste. Katie had a chance to make it—they'd gotten to her while she was young enough, and she was bright and strong. But she was going to throw it away. Dropping group was just the first step, he knew. Unless he found a way to put a stop to it.

"Katie," he said, "I don't know who you're doing this for, and right now I don't care. All I know is, this is not what's best for you. And you know it too. You're sacrificing yourself for someone else and it's not a smart move."

She wouldn't look at him. She was staring out the window. He couldn't read her eyes.

"You're going to have to fight for yourself, Katie. I wish you didn't have to. I wish you had all the support systems any kid is entitled to, but you don't. It isn't fair, but that's the way it is.

"The good news is, if you keep working the way you have been, you can get well. I believe that. I think you can have a good life. But not if you're sick. That much I can guarantee you."

She wanted to look at him, he could feel it. She wanted to break down and admit how much this terrible, painful sacrifice was costing her. But she wouldn't do it because she was so damn strong. It was her greatest liability and her greatest asset—her strength. And her mother had been trading on it for years. He was aware of a very unprofessional desire to hunt down Katherine Roskova and shake her, hard. Because he knew without question that she was behind this move.

But then the professional in him kicked in—God knows what problems Katherine has, he thought. Meanwhile, her daughter was sitting in front of him.

"The choice is yours, Katie. I can't make you get on your own team. But I will tell you that I want you to. I want that very much."

"DID SHE HEAR what you were saying?" his wife asked that night when he told her about his moment on the soapbox.

"Who knows?" said Sandy gloomily. "She's still not coming back to group."

"Maybe she'll reconsider later. She's not used to considering her own needs. Sometimes it takes a while for a new idea to sink in. At least now you've planted the seed."

He nodded. He knew he'd done his best, but still . . . "She just doesn't realize how serious her situation is. She thinks she can tough it out. And she's so good at taking pain, she probably can continue to function for quite a while. But when it finally falls apart . . ." He shook his head. "That kid is at risk—she really could slip through the cracks," he said.

"At least she's still in therapy," said his wife. "That's something."

"Yes. It's something."

39

Katie missed her group more than she believed would be possible. She'd be walking through the halls at school and suddenly the realization that she would never see the girls again would hit her so strongly it would take everything she had not to sit down and cry. It felt as if someone had died. And she couldn't even mourn her loss because she'd brought it on herself.

Of course it got worse as the black hole of her day—otherwise known as lunchtime—approached.

Since her run-in with Dave and his friends in the parking lot, she'd been spending her lunch hours hiding out in the school library. It wasn't a good choice because it was directly across the hall from the cafeteria; however, there weren't a lot of other options.

One day shortly after she'd made her announcement to Sandy, she sat at a long, battered table in the empty library and looked out the window. The cheerful din caused by two hundred–plus kids socializing at the top of their lungs made her ache. She allowed her mind to indulge in a daydream she'd started right after she left her group, which had quickly become her favorite. It had to do with her sixteenth birthday, which was one week away.

Katie had known for some time that the others in the group often got together outside Sandy's office. Sometimes they met for lunch at the food court in the mall on Saturdays. Every once in a while after the weekly session they'd all go to a nearby coffee shop for sodas. They always invited her to come along but she hadn't even bothered to ask Katherine if she could because she'd known what the answer would be.

But her birthday would be different—at least, it was in her daydream. She and the girls would meet at a restaurant—she wasn't sure which one yet, the details were still a bit hazy. Izzy and Jodi would insist on sitting in the smoking section. Beth would give them a hard time about that. Izzy would tell her to get a life.

Katie would bring a cake she'd had decorated at a bakery with big, pink, goopy roses. And the waitresses would sing "Happy Birthday." It would be too corny and dumb for a girl who was sixteen, but her friends would understand that she wanted it because she'd never had a real birthday party. They'd kid her, but they'd understand.

Except . . . they weren't her friends anymore because she had exiled herself from their circle. So she had to stop the fantasy. Because if she let herself imagine it anymore, she'd get angry. And she'd resent Katherine. Which would defeat the whole purpose of giving up the group in the first place.

She turned away from the window. Two kids had come into the library while she was daydreaming. They were a boy and a girl—a couple she recognized from her geometry class. Now they were sitting next to each other at a table, studying. The boy was casually rubbing the girl's neck with the back of his hand. Then, without warning, he reached over and kissed her on the mouth. The girl leaned back slightly in her chair and pulled him to her. It was the ease of it that took Katie's breath away. They just did it—simply and naturally. There was something almost cozy about it. When they stopped kissing, they went back to whatever they had been studying without saying a word. The boy was rubbing the girl's neck again with his hand.

Katie wondered what it would be like to have someone you could kiss like that whenever you wanted to . . . just because you wanted to. She wondered what it would be like to be kissed. It was one of her shameful secrets that she didn't know. She was almost sixteen years old and she'd never been kissed by a boy.

Suddenly she couldn't stand being in the library anymore. She packed up her books and left.

DAVE AND JOSH were in the parking lot—the buddy whose name she couldn't remember didn't seem to be around. She saw the two guys before they saw her and for a moment she hesitated. She'd never really talked to a boy before—not a boy she was attracted to. Well, it's about time, she said to herself. Get a life, stupid. She walked toward Dave and Josh.

As she got closer, she saw that this time Dave and Josh were passing the bottle back and forth. Josh was the one who spotted her.

"Look what showed up, man," he said to Dave. He didn't bother to hide the bottle. "Cherry-picking time," he added with a snicker. Katie felt herself blush—because of his tone more than what he'd said. Although she was pretty sure she knew what he meant. But she kept on walking to them.

Dave's reddish gold hair glinted in the sunshine.

"Hey," she said to him. Her voice was steady, it hadn't gotten high or shaky, which was good. "Are you still offering that car ride?" she asked.

Dave looked her over slowly. There was a flicker of something like amusement—or contempt—in his eyes. Her mind flashed to her mom saying that Jodi and Izzy were cheap. She didn't care. She gave him her best winner's smile.

"Maybe," he said finally. "Do you like to go fast?"

Josh hooted with laughter and gave Dave a high five. Katie wondered if they were drunk. For a moment, she was afraid. But it didn't matter. There was no turning back from this. She felt almost the way she did when she knew she was going to use the scissors. She had to do it.

"Sounds like fun," she said casually.

Dave opened the car door. "Get in," he said.

Josh gave another one of his hooting laughs and started for another car, which Katie assumed was his. Dave grabbed the bottle from him. "Get your own booze," he said. He got into the driver's seat.

"Want some?" he asked, indicating the bottle.

She shook her head.

He took a drink while she watched. He seemed to feel he owed her an explanation. "I ripped the shit out of my knee during training last season," he said. "I didn't want Coach to know because he would have benched me. A little Stoli takes the edge off."

"I understand," she said. "I've never hurt my knee, but I've skated on a bad ankle." It was such a dumb thing to say. But she couldn't think of anything else. Dave looked at her as if she were from another planet. "So what?" he asked.

"I'm just saying that in my sport—"

"Your sport?" he cut her off. "What sport?"

He had to know she was a skater. Everyone at school did. "Figure skating, of course."

He laughed. "That's not a sport. That's a bunch of faggots dancing around on ice."

"A lot of people like figure skating," she said tentatively. "It's the second most popular sport on television."

Why was she having this stupid conversation with him? After all the times she'd thought about being alone with him—all the important things she'd planned to say—why was she blowing it like this?

But Dave didn't seem to notice how dumb she was being. "Okay," he said. "I'll make a deal with you. Next time you go skating, you take me along. If you wear one of those short little skirts that doesn't cover your ass, I might even watch you without falling asleep."

He took another pull at the bottle and rammed it into a soft-drinks holder that was connected to the dashboard. Katie wanted to ask him not to drink any more. But she was afraid he might get mad at her. Then he turned and grinned at her and she was glad she hadn't.

"So you like to go fast," he said.

She nodded gamely and started to fasten her seat belt. Dave hadn't fastened his. "What's the matter, are you chicken?" he asked softly.

She forced her hands not to shake as she unfastened the

belt. She smiled brightly. "I'm not afraid of anything," she said.

He reached over and turned on his radio. Loud, angry music poured out. "We'll see," he shouted over the noise.

At the other end of the parking lot, Josh had gotten into his car. He gunned his engine and sped off. Seconds later she and Dave followed him.

THE TOP OF Dave's convertible was down; the sun was beating on her, and the music was blaring. Josh was in front of them, heading out of the center of town to an area where the single-lane roads twisted through the countryside. Suddenly Dave floored the gas pedal, passing Josh, who screamed an obscenity as they went by him.

IT WAS A TEST—that she knew right away. If she didn't gasp when he took the curves so fast that the car skidded, she would pass it. If she didn't scream when he flew past an oncoming van with inches to spare, he might like her. She had to endure this wild ride to earn his approval.

And she could do it. She knew how to smile when she was frightened—it was like turning off your mind when you were in pain. She'd been doing it all of her life. That was how you skated your first competition on a sprained ankle that was so swollen they had to cut your boot off your foot after you won. You turned off your mind. That was how you did jumps and spins at speeds that terrified you, how you whipped yourself around the ice faster and faster. You turned off your mind and you waited out the pain and the fear. Because you knew it wouldn't last forever. "This will be over soon," said the voice in her head. And the prize would be worth it.

"You like this?" Dave shouted.

She forced herself to nod. This will be over soon, this will be over soon, she chanted inside her head.

Dave laughed. "You really are crazy," he yelled.

Josh was trying to pass them again. "No damn way, man," Dave shouted over the wind. They raced along the road neck and neck. This-will-be-over-soon-this-will-be-over-soon-this-will-be-over-soon, went the mantra inside her head.

A car was coming up ahead of them, directly in line to hit Josh. If he cut in front of them she would go through the windshield—there would be shards of glass and blood and hundreds of cuts—not on her arms where it was safe—cuts on her face—in her eyes.

Katie braced herself against the dashboard as the other car swerved at the last second and Josh fell in behind them. She was still clutching the dashboard when Dave glanced over and saw her.

"Thought you weren't afraid," he yelled over the music and the wind that was roaring by. "What's the matter, crazy girl, don't you trust me?" He was jeering at her now. "I trust you. Look." He pulled his hands off the wheel and turned to her. The look on his face was ugly. "You drive, crazy Katie. You take the wheel."

She couldn't move, she was frozen. This-will-all-be-over-soon-this-will-all-be-over-soon.

"Come on. Drive." His voice taunted her over the sound of the music and the wind.

Finally her chest exploded and a sound came out.

"Stop!" she screamed at him. "Stop! Stop! Stop!"

Her voice, high and loud, was drowned out by the wailing of the police siren behind them.

40

The first thing was, she mustn't cry. So far she'd been good. She'd stayed dry-eyed when the police stopped them and when they'd put the handcuffs on Josh and Dave. She'd fought the tears successfully when they'd put her in the backseat of the squad car and driven her to the police station. She hadn't even cried with relief when they told her they were going to release her because she wasn't the one who had been drinking.

"We're not gonna hold you, you're free to go," the pudgy cop behind the desk had said. "Just do yourself a favor. Don't hang around with that Malloy kid anymore. He's gonna get himself in real trouble someday. If he doesn't kill himself first. Now call your parents and tell them to get you outta here."

But she couldn't call Katherine. Because then she'd start crying and she wouldn't be able to stop. So she had to find someone else to pick her up.

Luck was on her side because Katherine was interviewing a new skating coach that day after work. So if she could just find someone to get her home before Katherine arrived . . .

JENNY MORAN was about to leave school for the day when the school secretary called her into the main office to take a phone call from one of her students.

NOW HOW DO I handle this, Jenny wondered as she led Katie out of the police station to her car. Dave and Josh were still inside, presumably awaiting the arrival of Dave's father's lawyer who, according to Dave, would "ream the asses" of the police who had had the temerity to spoil his fun.

When Jenny had arrived at the station asking for Katie, the cop at the desk had referred to her as Mrs. Roskova. Jenny hadn't corrected him. She'd been perfectly willing to lie and pose as Katherine Roskova if that was what it took to get the child out of there. But now she and Katie had a problem.

She got into her car and motioned for Katie to get in next to her. "You do realize that I have to tell your mom about this, don't you?" she asked.

Katie didn't answer.

The girl who sat beside her was a sharp contrast to the bright, smiling Katie she'd once known. This kid was bedraggled and beaten-looking. She slumped in her seat in the classic pose of adolescents everywhere. Still, Jenny's instinct told her that this new, raw-edged Katie was much more accessible than the golden girl had been.

"I have my own theory about why you were out joyriding with Dave and Josh during the middle of a school day," Jenny said, "but I'd love to hear your explanation."

Katie looked at her. For a moment, Jenny thought she was going to get another one of the kid's carefully crafted, slick non-answers; instead, she turned away again.

"I don't know why I did it," she muttered.

"Not good enough, Katie."

"It's all I know."

"You brought me into this, you owe me an explanation."

"I can't tell you why I did it, okay? I can't tell you why." She burst into tears. Jenny resisted the impulse to comfort her.

"I was so scared," Katie sobbed. "I knew they'd been drinking, but I got in the car anyway. And then when they started racing . . ." She turned dark, haunted eyes to Jenny. "Ms. Moran, I wasn't even wearing my seat belt. I could have gotten killed . . . But I couldn't ask him to stop and let me out of the car. He took his hands off the wheel to scare me, and I didn't know how to tell him he couldn't do that to me. I couldn't stand up for myself. Even if it meant I died." She was sobbing like a lost child now. Jenny put her arms around her and let her cry it out.

Finally, Katie pulled back. "I'm sorry," she said.

"Don't be. I was just thinking that you've come such a long way."

Katie looked off into space, and Jenny saw her struggle to get her next words out. Finally, she said, "I think the reason I did what I did today . . ." She drew a deep, shuddery breath. "I have a few problems . . . ," she began, then stopped. "No," she said. "It's not just a few problems." She turned to look directly at Jenny with the kind of fierce honesty teenagers could sometimes muster. "I am sick," she said slowly and clearly. "I am sick emotionally."

"But I think the good part is, you know you're in trouble and you're working on yourself."

Katie gave her a small, grudging nod. "I don't understand it all yet," she said.

"Doesn't it take time to figure it out?"

Katie nodded. "I guess." She looked at Jenny and smiled. It wasn't her old dazzler; this smile was weary. "It's just . . . I'm so tired of being crazy," she said softly.

She was so sad. No kid her age should be that sad. "Just keep going the way you are, Katie, and you'll make it."

For the first time since she'd gotten into the car, Katie seemed to brighten. "That's what my shrink says," she said. "He believes in me." She leaned back and closed her eyes. "Do you really have to tell my mom?" she asked.

"Since I'm your teacher, the school wouldn't want me to keep this from her." Jenny paused. "Besides, I think she should know. I think she needs to know. I'll come with you if you like."

"Thanks."

41

Her mom was on a roll. "My Katie was in the police station?" she yelled. "Why didn't you people keep her on the school grounds? Isn't that your job?"

"We don't have time to watch each student individually," Ms. Moran said reasonably. Katie could have told her she was wasting her breath. Reason never worked when Katherine was on the warpath.

"Besides," Ms. Moran continued, "I don't think we should look at this as an isolated incident. It's more of an indicator of the difficulties Katie's facing—"

"Katie only has one 'difficulty.' That shrink you and the people at the school made me take her to. He's the one who's causing the 'difficulties.' That man has been turning Katie against me. He tells her to talk back to me, and fight with me. He puts her in a crowd of girls who dress like hookers and probably aren't any better than they look. No wonder she's started getting into trouble."

"You can't blame Katie's therapy for what happened today," said Ms. Moran.

"Can't I? Katie never did anything like this before. She never cut classes to ride around with drunken bums. She was never picked up by the police. You think it's just a coincidence that this happened after she started going to that quack?"

"Ms. Roskova, Katie needed help—"

"Well, thanks to you she got it. And today she almost got arrested." Her mother took a deep breath. "Maybe you meant well," she said, "but from now on I'll take care of my daughter." With that she stalked to the front door and opened it. "Thank you for bringing Katie home," she said.

Ms. Moran hesitated; Katie could tell there was more she wanted to say. But Katherine was making it clear that the conversation was over.

"If you need me, you know how to reach me, Katie," Ms. Moran said. Then she left.

"THAT DOES IT," said her mother when they were alone. She walked into the kitchen and began pulling things out of the refrigerator for dinner. Katie followed quickly. "I'm not putting up with that school anymore," said Katherine. "And I'm not putting up with that shrink."

"They say I have to go to him," Katie said nervously. Even talking about leaving therapy made her feel shaky.

"I'm not worried about them anymore. We don't need them." Katherine turned to her. The surprise was, instead of being angry, her mom was smiling. "Katie, I've thought it all through. I wasn't going to tell you until your birthday. It was going to be a surprise. But now that all of this has happened . . ." She paused; her eyes were sparkling. Katie thought she'd never seen her so happy. "What would you say if I told you you'd never have to go back to that school again? What if I said we were going to leave New Rochelle and move up to Connecticut to be near that new skating complex?"

It was as if she were trying to watch a videotape that someone was fast-forwarding, Katie thought. She couldn't follow what was happening because it was going by so quickly. "Why would we do that?" she asked.

"Because I've talked to Miralen Laird about taking you on, and that's where she works."

Laird was one of the best coaches around. She was also one of the hardest. Her skaters were known to be barracudas, and she enjoyed fostering competition among them. "I don't have a stable of athletes," she liked to say to interviewers, "I have a shark tank."

"I did quite a selling job, if I do say so myself," said

Katherine proudly. "Miralen was worried because she usually doesn't take girls who are as old as you are. But I convinced her to let you work with her on probation for a few months. Then she'll make her decision. This is the break we've been waiting for, Katie. If she takes you on, you've got it made."

"But what about the academy?"

"I told you, you'll be leaving that miserable hole. The place has gone sour on you. Wouldn't you like to make a fresh start?"

"But where would I go? We need a scholarship for private school, and the public schools will give us a hard time about my schedule."

"Katie, Katie, you're not thinking," her mother said playfully. "Next week you turn sixteen. Remember what happens then?"

The only thing that came to mind was the fact that she'd be old enough to get a driver's license. But that was not what was making her mother so excited. "You'll be free, Katie," said Katherine blithely. "Legally free. No one can force you to go to school anymore."

"But . . . my graduation . . . my high school diploma . . ."

"Oh, for heaven's sake, what do you need with a high school diploma if you're in training with Miralen Laird? Besides, if you really want that stupid piece of paper, you're smart, you can pick up your GED someday with a correspondence course. Right now you have to concentrate on your skating. You've lost valuable time these last few months."

"I can do both," Katie said frantically. "I can catch up with my skating and stay in school."

"The people at that school are making too many demands on you. They're distracting you. This is our chance to get rid of them."

But she couldn't lose the school. Because without the threat from Westchester Academy, there was something else Katherine would want to get rid of.

"What about my therapy?"

"You're going to be much too busy to bother with that."

It couldn't happen. She wouldn't let it. "But, Mom, I need to be in therapy," she said.

"That's ridiculous. You need to focus on training with Miralen. This is serious business, Katie."

"But my therapy is serious too."

"Your therapy is crap!" The happiness was gone from her mother's face now. And it was all her fault.

"What are you trying to do?" Katherine cried out in despair more than anger. "Do you want to ruin this?"

"No, Mom, but I need help."

"Why? Because your English teacher says you do? You listen to that Ms. Moran more than you do to me. She's more important to you than your own mother."

Everything was getting foggy. When she was in Sandy's office she knew who she was and what she needed. Her feelings were clear then. But now all she could feel was her mother's anger. And the pain that was under it.

"No, Mom. She's not."

"Then why did you call her today? You called her instead of me."

There it was—her betrayal and her guilt. She'd been wondering why Katherine hadn't said anything about it before.

"You turned to her," Katherine went on. "Do you know how that makes me feel?"

Katie knew. She bowed her head.

"She tells you you have difficulties and you need help and you believe her."

She pushed the fogginess away. She tried to remember what it felt like to sit in Sandy's office.

"Mom, Ms. Moran saw me go crazy in the hall . . ."

"She saw you lose your temper. Listen to me, Katya . . ." Katherine's voice took on a gentle, soothing tone. And when was the last time her mother had called her by that pet name? When she was five? Six? The fog was turning into a blur. "The people at that school don't understand you. They got scared because you're not like all the boring little nobodies they teach every day. You're special, Katya. You're a star."

The fogginess was taking over. Remember what it feels like to be in Sandy's office, she tried to tell herself.

"So sometimes you're a little too emotional," Katherine went on in her gentle, lullaby voice. "That's because you feel things deeply. They want to take that away from you. That's why they want you to go to that therapist. Because they want you to be like everyone else. But I'm not going to let them do that to you."

It was so hard to hang on to the memory of feeling clear. It would be so much easier to give in to the fogginess. Especially now that the fog was starting to blur and shimmer.

"Trust me, Katie," her mother was saying. "Do you trust me?"

She was going to say yes. She was going to stop fighting and say yes to her mother. She had to.

But she didn't. Instead she watched herself get up and walk across the kitchen.

"Katie, what are you doing?" Katherine asked.

"Nothing, Mom," she said. "I'm not doing anything."

But she was doing something. She was moving to the counter where the knife rack was. And she was pulling back the sleeve of her blouse.

Her mother's face was receding. "Katie, what are you doing?" she called out again from a growing distance.

The knives were so much bigger than her scissors. Even the smallest one was. But that was all right. She could manage. She pulled the knife out of the rack.

"Katie?" Her mother's voice was far away now. But not so far that she couldn't hear the panic in it.

"It's just a little performance, Mom," said the voice inside her head. "You like to watch me perform." She held her arm out from her body so Katherine could see it. She brought the blade to it slowly and carefully. She heard Katherine gasp. She cut hard—no little nick this time. The blood welled up immediately, bright red. Katherine started to scream. Katie put the knife to her arm again—the show wasn't over. Watch me, Mom, she silently commanded her mother. Watch me make a big, long cut just for you. This is what I do. See it, Mom? This is what I am. This is what I'll always be.

But then suddenly the hand that was holding the knife stopped. Because that wasn't what she was. Not anymore. Now she was the girl who had friends named Izzy and Jodi and Beth and Elsie and Pam. She was the girl who cuddled Satchie. She was the girl who could talk to Sandy about anything.

The knife blade was at her skin. Soon the hand would cut again. But for the first time, she didn't want it to. Because she didn't want to bleed. And she didn't want to feel the pain.

"You have to fight for yourself," Sandy had said. "You have to get on your own team."

"Katie, stop this," Katherine was screaming.

"I'm tired of being crazy," she'd told Ms. Moran.

"Katie," her mother screamed.

Yes, I'm Katie. I'm Katie Roskova, I know who I am. And I don't want to hurt myself anymore.

IN THE END, she couldn't stop what she'd started. But the second cut was very small. And then she did put down the knife.

42

"So how are you and your mom now?" asked Sandy the next day during the special session Katie had asked for.

"What with one thing and another, she's a little frightened of me at the moment," Katie said dryly. Sandy had noticed that she'd been developing a nice deadpan delivery when she wanted to be funny. He had a feeling they were about to go into a major Dorothy Parker phase.

"I bet she is," he said lightly. "Sounds like you were pretty scary."

"I scared myself." No deadpan delivery now. She was serious.

"I'm glad to hear it," he said just as seriously.

"For now my mom says she'll pay for therapy with you. But when she gets over being afraid . . . I'm not so sure what she'll do . . ."

"Katie, don't write scripts for your mom. See what she does. Whatever happens, you and I will find ways to deal . . ."

"But if I can't afford to go on . . ."

"I've been known to make financial arrangements with patients who need help."

She nodded. "Izzy says she thinks she knows a place where I could get a job this summer. I'd like to earn some money. I think it would make me feel"—she struggled with the word which was a taboo for her—"independent. You know?"

Sandy nodded. There was no need for her to say that it was her mother from whom she would be winning her independence. Little steps, Katie, he thought. This process goes in little steps.

"Of course, if I work, it would interfere with my skating time . . ."

"And how does . . ."

". . . that make me feel?" she finished the sentence for him and they both laughed. "I don't know. I still love to skate. But I don't love the pressure. And Mom's right, if I don't make a big commitment to it soon, it'll be too late." She sighed. "Everything's up in the air right now. I don't know if they'll take me back at Westchester Academy if I'm not a skater. And I'm not sure I want to go back. It's not as though I have lots of friends there. The only person I'd really miss would be Ms. Moran . . ."

"I'm sure she'd stay in touch even if you left the school."

And in a couple of years, if you get a healthy life going for yourself with friends your own age, you won't miss any adult very much, including me, he thought. At least, that's what I'm hoping will happen for you. He saw that she was frowning.

"What is it, Katie?"

"Last night . . . I couldn't keep from cutting myself, even though I wanted to stop . . . I don't think I'm through hurting myself . . ."

"No, this stuff with the mind goes much more slowly than that. But it is a start . . ."

She nodded.

43

They weren't at a fancy restaurant with tablecloths, it was just the coffee shop that was down the street from Sandy's office building. And they didn't do it on her birthday, they went there after her first session back in group. There wasn't a special cake with roses either. But that was okay. Because all of them came—her entire group. Jodi and Beth gave her a signed pledge that they would teach her how to drive. And the rest of them gave her a T-shirt that said "Shit Happens." Then Izzy ordered a corn muffin, stuck a candle in it, and lit it.

"You have to blow out the candle for luck," she said. Katie nodded, drew in a big breath, and extinguished the small flame. But she knew she didn't need to blow out candles for luck—not now. Because at that moment, she felt like the luckiest girl in the world.

Izzy, Jodi, Beth, Pam, and Elsie leaned in to sing softly so they wouldn't disturb the other customers. "Happy birthday to you . . ." sang her friends.

"Happy birthday, dear Katie . . .

"Happy birthday to you . . ."

ABOUT THE AUTHOR

SINCE 1970, Steven Levenkron has treated anorexics as part of his full-time psychotherapy practice in New York City. He has held positions in many hospitals in the New York metropolitan area, among them, clinical consultant at Montefiore Hospital and Medical Center, clinical consultant at The Center for the Study of Anorexia and Bulimia in New York City, and adjunct director of the Eating Disorder Service at Four Winds Psychiatric Hospital in Westchester, New York. Currently he is a member of the advisory board of The National Association of Anorexia Nervosa and Associated Disorders (ANAD) in Highland Park, Illinois.

His 1978 novel, *The Best Little Girl in the World,* was made into an ABC-TV "Movie of the Week" in 1981. He is also the author of *Treating and Overcoming Anorexia Nervosa, Kessa,* and *Obsessive-Compulsive Disorders.*

Steven Levenkron lives in New York with his family.